Dark Revelation

by

S. E. MYERS

Dark Revelation – © S. E. Myers
Cover created by Nikki Fortugno
Edited by Todd Brown @ maydecemberpublications.com

Second Edition

ISBN-13: 978-1470088064
ISBN-10: 1470088061

This book is dedicated to my children - Illeana,

Gavin, and Kathryn.

You are the air that I breathe. I love you!

Acknowledgements

This book would not have been possible without the loving and unconditional support of my children, family, and friends. I appreciate the encouragement that I received throughout the creation of this novel. Self-doubt reared its ugly head and in those moments, you were there, offering the words I needed to hear. I would have never completed this without you. I love you all!

To the following people I wish to extend a special acknowledgement:

Nikki, thank you for creating such an amazing cover. Your creativity and friendship is unending.

Cheryl & the Elliott Clan, you have been the best friend anyone could ever hope for. Your love and advice have been invaluable. I love you.

To a select few from my former HomEq family, you know who you are, we have been able to move on and create new lives that resulted from chaos. I wish all of you the best in your future endeavors.

My New Jersey Devils, I am so glad I have you in my life. You are an amazing family and I am glad to be part of it.

Brice and Katie, thank you for all of your input. Brice, thank you for your eyes.

Mom and Michelle, I love you and miss you every day!

My Ward family, thank you for your support, love, and kindness. I am so grateful you are in my life.

Punky and Snoopy, you are my personal imps!

Author's Note: Throughout the creative process for this novel, music became a vital source of inspiration. Every writer has a moment in which they have to take the time to reflect on the progress of their work-in-progress and shake their brain. For those moments, I used music to give me that extra push and assist with the creation of imagery. Music has always helped me to write.

The playlist below is not all inclusive, but it contains some of my favorite songs and bands. I've labeled it, Ryleigh's Playlist; because I believe that she would also enjoy it.

Thank you,
S. E. Myers
Ryleigh's Playlist

Labyrinth – Oomph!
Only in my Mind – Imperative Reaction
How Can You Sleep? – Assemblage 23
When I'm not Around – Iris
Shake it Out – Florence + the Machine
Side Effect – Imperative Reaction
I Won't Tell You – Lacuna Coil
Stigmata – Omega Lithium
Face Up – LIGHTS
Time is Running Out – Muse
Frozen Oceans – Shiny Toy Guns
Hysteria – Muse
Damaged – Assemblage 23
Judith – A Perfect Circle
Vyrisus – Skinny Puppy
The Farthest Star – VNV Nation
The Art of Revenge – XP8
Dead Enough for Life – Icon of Coil
House of Cards – Zeromancer
V – Zeromancer
No Light, No Light – Florence + the Machine
Rocking Horse – Coda

Table of Contents

1

A tragedy is how it always starts

Her feet pounding on the pavement kept time with the music streaming through her headphones. While her chest burned with each gulping breath, her legs threatened to stop moving, but Ryleigh Simmons didn't know the meaning of the word *quit*. Sheer determination flowed through her body and continued to propel her forward. Sweat dripped down her forehead threatening to flood her eyes. Brushing back the droplets and an escaped strand of her ebony hair, she continued to run.

This was her daily routine – to get up and run. It helped release the stress that built beneath her quiet exterior. Outwardly, she looked as undisturbed as a secluded pond; however, one stone's throw could perpetuate an outward ripple that threatened violence.

Her father taught her how to release the caged animal inside her through exercise…and running was the way of it.

Ryleigh had always been a bit of a hothead. From the time she entered social situations with other children, she had a tendency to find trouble. Her overreaction ended up with the other child crying, bleeding, and bruised. Her parents ended up with a concerned phone call. By the time Ryleigh was in third grade, she was made to see a therapist for her outbursts and lack of control. Refusal to do so would result in Child Protective Services being called. Ryleigh's father Tom knew that the type of therapy offered would do little for his daughter; so…running it was.

As she ran, he would walk. "It's for your own good," he would reassure. At first Ryleigh resisted. She hated it and loathed him. At eight years old, she would rather play with her dolls than run. As time progressed and she became older, it became a part of her everyday life. Something she couldn't do without. The more she ran, the calmer she felt, the easier it was to function -- normally. By the time Ryleigh was in 5th grade, her outbursts slowed to a trickle as long as she expended the energy that grew from the deep well within her.

Ryleigh usually woke at five a.m. to run every day. Except today. Today was her seventeenth birthday and she treated herself to an extra hour of sleep. A six a.m. run. She enjoyed the crisp mornings in the New Mexico desert. As the seasons progressed, she witnessed the sun rise in its splendor, changing the colors of the desert to an O'Keeffe painting.

Prior to living in New Mexico, her family moved around - a lot. Her father's work moved them often. Promotions, department changes, the varied reasons were of little consolation.

She also knew that, when her mother started baking, it was time to move. Her mother only started to bake when her stress levels peaked. There would be chocolate cakes, cookies, and pies for days. Her mother always said that sweets made stress easier. For Ryleigh, running made stress easier. After moving for the umpteenth time in her life to New Mexico, her father promised this would be permanent. It was the last place her family would be moving for a long time.

Before she knew it, time would fly and she would be ready to head off to college. Ryleigh was looking forward to the coming summer before the start of her senior year.

This summer, her family would vacation in Yosemite. They were planning a two week camping trip. Just the three of them. Ryleigh was excited, and her father had begged the time off work specifically to spend with the family. He was almost always gone. Usually it was Ryleigh and her mom alone all the time.

Ryleigh's mind drifted to what she would do during their two week hiatus. She was definitely looking forward to the campfire S'mores. Rounding the block to her house on Ashford Drive, she saw her father's car in the driveway.

She waved to her dad as his face erupted into a large smile. "There's my girl." Tom Simmons' blue eyes shone with excitement. He was proud of the woman his daughter was becoming.

Father and daughter looked alike: raven hair, fair complexion
– the only difference between them being their eye color. While his
were a bright blue, hers were sea foam green.

Ryleigh stopped short of him jogging in place and breathing
heavily. "I didn't…expect you…home so early!" Ryleigh said in
between breaths.

"Yeah, I got an early flight out today. Gotta get ready for our
trip tomorrow!" her father said as he enveloped her sweaty body in a
tight hug.

"Ugh! Dad!" Ryleigh exclaimed pushing him back and
smoothing down her clothes. "I am so disgusting right now." Tom
laughed. His laugh was a musical belly laugh that shook his slender
body. Ryleigh laughed with him and they walked into their house.

"Honey, I'm home," Tom announced. Adrianne, Ryleigh's
mother, came out from the kitchen. She was already up trying to
figure out the menu for the camping trip.

"Tom, I am so glad you are home!" Ryleigh's parents
embraced warmly.

Ryleigh rolled her eyes and walked upstairs. "I am getting in
the shower while you two lovebirds become reacquainted. Yuck."
She could hear soft laughter behind her as she went up the stairs to
her room to change.

In the shower, Ryleigh used the time to think. She didn't
have a lot of friends that she kept in touch with from the places that
she lived in before. She didn't have much of any social life to be

honest. She spent most of her time immersed in books, movies, and video games; that was her lifestyle.

She did have one friend…one friend that she'd made once her family had moved to New Mexico: Cyrus Davidson—tall, blonde, lanky, and mildly good looking. He was her neighbor, and he was her *only* friend. During the time that they lived next door to each other—which were the last six months—their friendship had blossomed into a lifetime bond. She knew that he had romantic intentions toward her, but she didn't want to ruin the friendship she had with him. Besides, she'd never had a boyfriend. Ever. Never kissed anyone. She'd never even had a best friend. Not that she could remember.

The streaming hot water was comforting to Ryleigh. Never once had she ever taken anything other than a hot shower. She wasn't sure why the warmth comforted her so much. She knew that she never wanted to live in a cold climate. The time they lived in Canada was the worst experience of her life. It was so cold she couldn't move. Her father transferred after only a few months of living there. That's when they moved to New Mexico and committed to only living in warm states.

Done with the shower, Ryleigh threw on her favorite pair of well-worn jeans, black t-shirt, and purple flannel. She hurried downstairs to go hang out with Cyrus. He'd just bought a new game and wanted to play co-op. She stopped short when she saw her mom and dad in deep conversation. A funny feeling traveled her spine, and she had an inkling that they were talking about her.

Her mom spotted her and sat up from the couch. "Ryleigh honey, what are your plans for the day?" her mother asked.

"I'm just going over to Cy's to hang out. We're going to play this new game that he picked up at midnight last night that we've been waiting for *forever*."

Her mom nodded. "Okay, just don't melt your brain!" A familiar phrase Ryleigh heard time and time again while playing video games. Her mother consistently played the concerned parent when Ryleigh became too involved with technology of any form. Ryleigh nodded and ran out the back door, cutting around the side of the house.

Cyrus's house was a refuge away from home. She enjoyed being over there as much as she possibly could. His house was the mirror floor plan of hers, including his room. Coming around the front of the house, and hopping over the short fence that divided their front yard, she noticed him sitting on his front porch.

"Thought you weren't going to make it today, Ry," Cyrus harassed Ryleigh often.

"And miss kicking your butt? Yeah, right!" Cyrus called Ryleigh 'Ry' and Ryleigh called him 'Cy'. They found it funny that their nicknames rhymed. *The Ry and Cy show.* Ryleigh and Cyrus headed into the house. She waved at his mom Shirley as they headed up to his room.

"Keep that door open!" she called up to them, knowing that nothing would ever happen between the two.

"I will mom!" Cyrus called down.

The pair headed into his room. He left the door cracked open behind him and they plopped into the twin bean bags in front of his small entertainment system.

"I am still jealous of the setup you have here," Ryleigh mentioned.

Her father refused to put a television in her room fearing he would never see his daughter emerge. He felt it was bad enough that he allowed her to have her laptop in her room with the amount of time that she spent on it. Her father wanted real interaction with his daughter.

"Don't be jealous, Ry, it was a buyoff from my mom because of how my dad left," Cy remarked.

"I know, Cy, I know. I remember."

A short time after Ryleigh moved next door, Cy's dad, Rodney, disappeared in the middle of the night. It was shocking news when he left his family. There wasn't any explanation; no note, not even a phone call.

Ryleigh reached over to comfort her friend. As they embraced, Cyrus's body stiffened as if each muscle in his body convulsed at the same time. He then relaxed into her arms. Ryleigh could feel a tingling sensation pulsate over her skin, and her heart started to beat faster. She wasn't sure what to do and attempted to break the hug, but Cyrus leaned into her more deeply. Ryleigh jumped up immediately. Cyrus looked at her with his eyes glazed over and a goofy grin.

"What are you doing?" she asked him.

He looked at her blankly for a moment. Regaining his composure as confusion masked his face he asked, "Wha-What just happened?"

"I'm-I'm not sure, but maybe you need to get a drink of water or something."

"Yeah. Yeah, maybe you're right," he agreed standing up slowly.

He made his way to the bathroom to get a drink of water giving Ryleigh a moment to think about what happened. Ryleigh was a little nervous and self-conscious. The urgency to leave pressed against her. She didn't want Cy to think that it was because of him so she restrained herself to stay for a little while. She decided that she would make an excuse to go back home after a while. He was her best friend after all.

Cy opened the bathroom door. "You know, I'm actually feeling a little sick. Can we play this when you get back? I promise I will wait."

Ryleigh was a little hurt and yet a little relieved at the same time. "Yeah, that's fine. I have to pack anyway."

Ryleigh got up to walk out of the room, and Cyrus went to grab her hand. Ryleigh jumped back. Afraid of the contact, she stumbled over the bean bag, fell backward, and landed on the floor. Cyrus just stood there staring at her.

"Are you okay?" he stammered.

"Mhmm, I'm fine. Just, uh, let me get up." Ryleigh pushed herself up from the floor avoiding touching Cyrus at all cost. "I promise I'll call you as soon as I get back."

"Sounds good, Ry."

"Hey, if you do play while I'm gone, don't spoil it for me, 'kay?"

"Alright," he replied meekly. "Take care of yourself. And-- Happy Birthday."

Ryleigh ran almost panicking from Cyrus's house to her own. She sped through the door and up the stairs before her parents could ascertain what was going on. Slamming her door, she threw herself onto her bed and buried her face into her pillow trying to understand what just happened.

A soft knock on the door was followed by her mother's concerned voice. "Ryleigh? Is everything okay?"

"Yeah, mom, I'm fine. It's just--Cy isn't feeling so great, so we are going to hang out when we get back from camping."

There was a short muffled conversation between her mom and dad behind the door. Ryleigh sat up on the side of her bed and walked to the door, pressing her ear into the wood attempting to hear the whispers of her parents', curious to know what they might have found out already about her little encounter.

"We should leave today," she could hear her mother telling her dad. "It's happening already."

"Alright, let me see what I can do and we'll go."

Ryleigh flung open her door. "Why do we need to leave today? I thought we were going to leave tomorrow?"

Her parents looked at her as if they were willing the words to come for an explanation. She could see it in their eyes. The words were there to give her a clue, but she wasn't picking it up.

Her dad was the first to speak. "When we get to the campsite we will talk. There is so much that we need to tell you."

Ryleigh's confusion was apparent as her facial features told the story. Her bright green eyes flashed with hurt and betrayal. They were always honest with each other and never kept secrets. But it seemed as if her parents were keeping a secret so huge, it would take a trip away from civilization for them to finally clue her in.

Adrianne reached out to embrace her daughter. Ryleigh flinched and turned away from her, skulking back inside her room. She thought about slamming the door in her parents' face for good measure, just so they could understand exactly how she was feeling.

"We are going to leave in a few hours," her mother advised, "Your dad and I will pack the car. You need to make sure you have everything ready to go. One last count for all items."

Ryleigh contained the scream building inside her and allowed only a single tear to make its escape. She grabbed her mp3 player, jammed the ear buds in her ears, and blasted the comforting melodic tones of her latest crush.

Ryleigh's bags were already stacked at the end of her vanity. She resigned herself to go through her bags and repack them once more. Going through her things and listening to her music kept her emotions in check. She used a methodical approach to the situation. She didn't allow for immature emotions to bubble up. Her father taught her that. If she didn't control her anger—things could get out of control. So instead, she concentrated on something else. The run that morning helped to ebb the emotional runoff, but she still had to work on suppressing it.

It took Ryleigh about an hour to finish going through her backpacks. She was bringing two normal-sized backpacks and one large bag. "Preparation is in the details" is what her father always said. She had a checklist that she created to double- and triple-check to ensure that all items were accounted for. Her family could not be faulted for lack of organization. They'd moved so many times, they developed the habit of checklists to verify everything was where it needed to be and also to ensure things got done the way they needed to be done.

Ryleigh headed downstairs with her bags and stopped at the bottom. She could hear her parents' muffled voices in the garage. She couldn't help the overwhelming feeling that the conversation was about her.

The moment Ryleigh entered the garage, the conversation stopped. The truck bed was packed with all the camping gear, waiting for the remaining personal items. Family camping was a ritual that they loved. Nature was a second home to her family. It didn't matter where, not really, they'd even camped in the desert from time to time. But this time, the mountains called to them.

"Oh, don't stop talking by my account," Ryleigh muttered under her breath.

Adrianne raised an eyebrow at the disrespectful tone she was getting from her daughter. "We are *not* going to have this attitude for the duration of our trip. You need to chill out."

"I am chill, mom," Ryleigh snarked back. "I just don't see why you can't say what's going on now and why we are leaving like we stole something!"

Tom laughed at his daughter's comment and then immediately sobered as he saw his wife's expression.

"Ryleigh, we just need to get out of here. The whole point of the camping trip was to have family bonding and talk about things that we need to. There are things that you need to know…especially now that you are seventeen. We just figured we would do it there."

Ryleigh just stared at her parents in disbelief. It was her birthday!

"Well, I guess there isn't any cake is there? Or are we waiting to celebrate my birthday camping instead of what we originally planned here. You know I had plans for today, I wasn't going to just stay in my room all day or with Cy playing games!" Ryleigh ended up almost screaming at her parents.

Her mother placed a cool hand onto her shoulder. "Ryleigh, that's enough. We are still going to celebrate, we are just going to do it on the road instead of at home. Okay?" Adrianne half implored.

Hot tears streamed down Ryleigh's face. What choice did she have really? She didn't have any other plans. She never had any other plans. The only thing she was going to do today was hang with her best friend. That was it. Ryleigh agreed and went back into the house to grab the rest of her things.

"Let her cool off, Tom," she could hear her mom telling her dad. "She is going to have to absorb a lot, and we need to allow her some space." Tom agreed and they resumed packing the truck.

Two hours later, they were on the road heading to Yosemite. Ryleigh sat in the back seat with her headphones in. She just wanted to listen to her music and not talk to anyone about anything at the moment. Before they took off, she talked to Cy one last time. It was an awkward conversation, but he looked like he was feeling better.

"I swear," Cy repeated, "I'm fine. We'll hang out when you get back." Ryleigh wasn't too convinced and thought she could hear a slight nervousness in his responses. He was her best friend and she trusted him. Implicitly.

Neither one of them knew or understood what happened to him, but they didn't hug or touch during the entire conversation. Ryleigh felt better that way. It was something that had never happened before. She would make sure it never happened again.

Closing her eyes she allowed the music in her ears and the rocking motion of the truck put her to sleep.

2

Bringing the dead back to life

He surveyed the wreckage before him. Twisted metal and the smell of burning oil and gasoline permeated his senses. The heat from the flames were intense. For once, he was glad that his imp was nosy. Obviously not nosy enough, or he could have prevented this from happening.

He spied her lying in the ruins of the accident. Running over to Ryleigh, his heart beat furiously in his chest hoping she was still alive. Anyone else happening upon the scene would assume her dead. She didn't have a pulse and didn't respond to physical stimuli. With her body surrounded by blood, and her skin a sickly pallor, the prognosis was not good. Tristan, however, could sense the energy still lingering within her. It hadn't dissipated and he knew that he could bring her back. The energy humming within her core was playing an old familiar song that only he could hear.

Ryleigh's injuries were devastating. She had multiple contusions and fractures. Tristan grimaced at the compound fracture in her right leg as he could see the gleaming white bone penetrating her skin. But the worst part…the worst of it was the three-foot metal rod impaling her chest.

"Shhh, it's okay. Everything is going to be alright," he said, knowing she couldn't hear him.

He felt a pop of air and his imp was beside him. "Vee, I'm going to need your help with this," he instructed.

The imp gazed at his master with his dark sparkling eyes. "We should not meddle, we should not meddle, Sir," he reminded.

"Meddling or not, this girl should not die. We need to save her. I need to save her," he implored.

The imp knew that, any order he was given, he had to comply. The imp placed his long fingers beneath Ryleigh's head. Tristan placed his hands, one on her chest beneath the injury and one on her stomach.

"Are you ready, Sir?" the imp asked his master.

"Yes," Tristan said closing his violet eyes.

The air stilled around the trio. A small violet flame erupted from Tristan's hand travelling outwardly encasing Ryleigh's body in a soft glow. The imp, who stood about two-feet tall, began to glow in the night as Tristan used him to channel energy into Ryleigh's beaten and broken body.

The sound of bones snapping into place echoed in the darkness. Ryleigh's body started to shake violently as it continued to heal. "Hold on, just hold on,"

Tristan pleaded. His eyes flashed open and the violet flames continued to glow even brighter. The rod impaling Ryleigh's chest began to move outward, and with each centimeter, the flesh and muscle behind it was being repaired.

"Master, we are not going to be able to finish," the imp said breathing heavily. "We can't fix it all. We can only do what is killing her."

Tristan nodded, and he focused on the metal piece protruding from Ryleigh's small, limp body. The last few inches of the metal rod came loose with a sickening wet sound and the wound closed up behind it.

As the rod fell to the ground, Ryleigh opened her eyes with a sharp breath. "Mom?" she asked.

Tristan brushed her hair, caressing her head with his hand. "Shhh, it's okay," he comforted again. He placed his hand on her forehead, "Sleep." Ryleigh closed her eyes and fell immediately to sleep.

Tristan, now completely exhausted, reached for his cellphone in the pocket of his pants and made the necessary phone call to 9-1-1.

Vee looked up at him, "Are you just going to leave her here, Master?"

"I have to for now," Tristan said, regretting the decision. "I have no choice…we can't bring her with us. She has additional wounds that need tending. But for now, she is out of immediate danger."

The imp nodded and they both disappeared as suddenly as they came.

3

In dreams are answers

Slowly starting to stir, she could hear the voices say, "Shhh, quiet – she's coming around." Ryleigh groaned as she attempted to open her eyes. "It's okay, little one, wake up," she could hear the soft voices calling to her.

Ryleigh opened her eyes and shut them immediately. The blinding light felt like fire raging through her skull. She could hear rustling around her. Opening her mouth to speak, her voice caught the gravel coating in the back of her throat. "Hello," she choked up.

Receiving no response, she attempted to open her eyes again. She slowly opened her eyelids until the light was bearable. Her body felt as if someone had used it as a punching bag. She attempted to sit up, but her arms didn't want to cooperate and felt as if she were moving through water in the deep end of the pool.

She made an attempt to call out to whomever was the in the room. "Hello?" she asked again. She could hear the soft tittering of voices.

Her vision still blurry, she could see small shadows to the right of her bed. "Can you help me? I can't seem to sit up." She heard the sharp intake of breath and then something that sounded like the reverse of the noise that a balloon makes when it is popped.

Ryleigh tried to sit up one more time. She felt an intense pain wrack her body from her toes to her head and lost consciousness.

* * *

She was dreaming. He had pale blue skin and white eyes. As he watched her, she could feel him penetrating her soul. She caught his glance with hers, and he smiled baring his razor sharp teeth.

Her skin started to tingle, and blue flame erupted, coating her in purple hues. She opened her mouth to scream, but no sound came out.

"Ryleigh," she heard. "Ryleigh, you need to wake up," the gentle voice coaxed her. Ryleigh opened her eyes and realized they didn't burn. It was dark as night. Her blurred vision cleared, and she turned toward the voice.

"Mom?" Ryleigh asked. Her eyes started to focus. A nurse was releasing the blood pressure cuff from Ryleigh's arm,

"No, sweetie, I am your nurse, Carol."

"Carol?" Ryleigh was confused. Her head was pounding, and she continued to feel pain travelling through her body in places she couldn't imagine. All she wanted were her parents, "Where is my mom?"

"I'll have the doctor come in just a minute," Carol said as she adjusted Ryleigh's IV line and walked out of the room.

Ryleigh's stomach sank, and she could feel her heart pounding through her chest. She tried to remember where she was and what she was doing. She knew she was in the hospital, but she couldn't remember why. Ryleigh's confusion reflected on the furiously beeping heart monitor.

A distinguished gentleman walked into her room preceded by Carol the nurse. "I'm Dr. Scarborough, Ryleigh." His bright eyes reflected kindness and Ryleigh didn't feel an ounce of threat. Dr. Scarborough walked to her bedside and grabbed her wrist measuring her pulse. "Well, it sounds like your heart is working."

Ryleigh looked up at him with confusion, "Wh-what is going on?"

Dr. Scarborough looked her in the eyes and gently asked, "What is the last thing you remember?"

She closed her eyes and attempted to remember the events as they unfolded from her memory. "I remember my mom, dad, and I were on our way to Yosemite. We were taking a vacation before the beginning of the school year. It was my birthday, and this was a birthday present to me because I like camping." The doctor nodded as she talked. Ryleigh opened her eyes suddenly. "Where's my mom?" she asked in a panic. "Where's my dad?" She started to get up out of bed.

Dr. Scarborough and Carol grabbed her arms. "Ryleigh, just breathe!" the doctor ordered.

But she couldn't breathe. Her heart felt as if it were going to burst from her chest. A sickening feeling continued to grow in the pit of her stomach. "Where are my mom and dad?" Ryleigh started to scream.

"NURSE!" the doctor yelled.

Carol grabbed a syringe and pushed it into her IV.

* * *

She was dreaming again. "Ryleigh." She heard whispers as she turned around examining where she was. She could feel him near her because her skin started to tingle again.

She wasn't sure where she was. A cave maybe? Crystals lined the walls sparkling like a disco ball illuminating a path before her. She heard her name again on the breeze as she continued forward.

An acidic smell permeated her nostrils. The smell of sulfur and sandalwood invaded her senses. Normally she would be repulsed; however, it intrigued her, pulling her deeper into the cave.

Rounding a corner, she caught a glimpse of pale blue skin. "Wait! Who's there?" she asked, stopping and standing still. She looked down at herself and she was in her hospital gown. Suddenly conscious of how naked she was, she started to shiver in a nonexistent breeze.

"Who are you? What do you want?" she asked with more force.

An almost non-existent voice answered her. "You know who I am."

"I don't. Tell me why I am here. Please?" she begged.

He stepped out of the shadows before her, sending Ryleigh into a terrified state. Her skin started to crawl as his eyes bore through her.

"Don't be scared," he said to her, moving closer. Ryleigh couldn't move even if she wanted to. It was as if her body was frozen by his gaze.

He was the most gorgeous creature she had ever seen in her life. At first, his skin appeared to be pale blue, yet, it became more translucent the closer he got to her. His hair was an absence of all color, however, it was his eyes that drew her in. They seemed to match his hair color, and she started to notice the violet and blue hue to the color. His pupils dilated with each step he took towards her. She wanted to scream and run away, but she was too enthralled with this creature in front of her. His gaze bore into her and she couldn't look away.

"Remember," was all he uttered.

With that, memories came flooding back to her. She remembered the accident. She remembered her mother screaming for her father and Ryleigh in the background. She remembered the

car flipping over and over and over again. She remembered the
pain from being impaled upon twisted metal from the accident. And
she remembered him. He was there helping her and soothing her
until the ambulance arrived. But he wasn't just soothing her.

Ryleigh grabbed her stomach, remembering the pain she felt,
feeling as if her insides were on fire and she couldn't breathe.
Before she asked anything further, her vision faded to black.

* * *

Ryleigh woke in her hospital room. She lay still for a
moment remembering the dream she just had and the visions of the
accident. Feeling a lump beginning to form in her throat she
swallowed it back down – hard. Although the emotions were raw
and on edge - now was not the time for tears.

Reaching for the nurses call button connected to the bed,
Ryleigh felt the urgent need to relieve her bladder. A pleasant
female tone crackled over the intercom, "I'll be right there."

"Thank you," Ryleigh croaked realizing how thirsty she was.
She sat up and examined her surroundings. The first thing she
noticed was the bouquets of flowers and balloons occupying almost
all of the vacant space. A giant poster board hung on the wall beside
her bed wishing her to get well soon by her classmates. She felt an
immense sense of appreciation and an overwhelming sadness.

A plump nurse walked in the room wheeling in a blood
pressure cuff and metal tray with a pitcher and a cup. Ryleigh
immediately felt grateful for her having the foresight to bring in

something that she desperately needed. But urgent needs took precedence.

"Okay, sweetie, how can I help you?" the nurse asked with her soft brown curls bobbing as she wrapped the cuff around Ryleigh's arm.

"I really – really need to use the restroom," Ryleigh implored.

The nurse looked at her with understanding and immediately took off the cuff. "Oh, okay, let me help you down." The nurse escorted Ryleigh to the restroom, making sure her legs were stable enough before letting her go on her own.

Still connected to the IV, Ryleigh had to wheel the contraption in with her. Once done, the nurse brought her back to the bed where a cup of water with a straw was waiting for her.

Ryleigh grabbed for the cup and the nurse cleared her throat. "You will want to take small sips at first or you will be sick." Ryleigh looked a little confused.

"Your stomach will not be used to the fluids and bounce it right back up."

Ryleigh nodded and took a small sip. The cold fluid was a welcome relief to her throat that felt as if it were the Sahara itself.

"The doctor will be in momentarily, okay, hon?" Ryleigh nodded with understanding and leaned back into her bed.

Feelings washed through Ryleigh as she remembered being told about her parents. She just lay in the bed absorbing how she felt, not knowing what was going to happen to her once she got out of the hospital.

Dr. Scarborough entered the room, and Ryleigh's stomach began to tighten. He smiled as he saw her, but she could see in his eyes it was an act.

"So, how are you doing today?"

Ryleigh answered, "I'm okay I guess. I can walk, and I am not feeling much pain."

Dr. Scarborough looked down Ryleigh's chart and then back at her. "Ryleigh, do you remember what happened?"

Ryleigh felt a knot in her throat too big to talk through, but somehow, she found the sound to choke out, "Yes."

The doctor approached Ryleigh kindheartedly and grasped her hand. "I know that this is very difficult for you. The loss of a parent is extremely hard, even on those this young, but you are healthy and alive. And, you do have family that is here waiting to meet you."

Wiping away an escaped tear, Ryleigh looked up at Dr. Scarborough. "I have family here? I didn't even know that I had family that existed."

She didn't have any other family that she could remember.

She never had family holidays or gatherings anywhere but with her parents, and on top of that, she was an only child. Her father and mother never talked about their parents...or even any brothers or sisters for that matter. Ryleigh couldn't remember her parents ever even having friends over to the house.

Dr. Scarborough looked towards the door, "You can come in now."

As soon as "you" spilled from his lips, in swooped a woman who looked nothing like Ryleigh would imagine anyone in her family to look like; she was wearing a blush colored couture suit with open-toed sling backs. Her blonde hair was done up in a French twist, and her eyes were so violet they were almost a translucent color. Tall, thin, and amazingly beautiful. She was nothing like Ryleigh had ever seen in real life.

"Ryleigh!" the woman exclaimed in a highly refined British accent, "I can't believe it's you!" She drew in close, smelling of lavender and sandalwood, sparking a distant memory in Ryleigh's brain.

"I'm sorry - but I don't know who you are," Ryleigh gasped as the woman embraced her in a loving hug.

"I am so sorry," the woman said, "My name is Vera. I am your aunt on your dad's side"
Ryleigh looked stunned.

"My aunt? I didn't even know my father had a sister," Ryleigh questioned.

"I know, darling, but I am here now and I am going to take care of you. You are going to stay with me and get out of this dreadful hospital."

Ryleigh wasn't sure what to make of this, but she knew that she did not want to go back to her home – that would remind her of her parents. Her memories lived there and that was something she could not deal with at this moment. She choked out an "Ok" and her aunt looked pleased.

Dr. Scarborough advised Ryleigh that she only needed a few more days in the hospital just to make sure. Aunt Vera fussed, saying that she had stayed long enough and she would speak with the hospital administrator if he didn't allow Ryleigh to leave. Dr. Scarborough looked a little surprised but acquiesced just the same. Aunt Vera always got her way and would never take "No" for an answer.

She turned smugly to Ryleigh and said," Now, dear, let's get you to your new home."

4

A new life...and new beginning?

Once she arrived at her new home, Ryleigh couldn't believe what she was looking at. Aunt Vera was not just beautiful, but, she was rich as her outfit indicated. And she just wasn't rich. She was extremely wealthy. Rich beyond Ryleigh's wildest imaginations. Ryleigh couldn't believe the size of her house.

Vera's home was replicated to look like a castle. She was a fan of renaissance Europe, medieval knights, and chivalry. It showed inside and outside of her home. Outside, the brick work and masonry were completed with exquisite attention to detail. Arched doors and corners to the home were built to look like watch towers. Large two-story windows were etched with stained glass artwork.

The front door custom built to seem as if thick wood and wrought iron was used in detail.

Ryleigh stood in the foyer half in disbelief as she marveled at the marble flooring. Her eyes continued to drink in her surroundings, mesmerized by it all. Never in a million years would she ever have imagined herself in a place like this. It made her a tad uncomfortable and placed her well beyond her own comfort zone.

Vera's butler, Siegfried, stood in the entryway. He turned clearing his throat, "Miss Ryleigh, this way to your room please." His direction was given as dryly as Ryleigh imagined a butler of this stature would say to her. As she followed Siegfried, she noticed that, for as old as he appeared, his countenance did not betray his age.

Ryleigh followed him up the stairs. She knew she would have more time to explore her surroundings – eventually. She was grateful to be out of the hospital and longed for a normal bed.

Siegfried led her upstairs to her room, and as she entered, she could feel her jaw drop. Her room could have fit into the one she was standing in at least three times over. The bed in the center of the room was twice the size of her old bed and covered by a pumpkin colored chiffon canopy that flowed like a waterfall over each of the bed posts. The furniture intentionally placed around the room enhanced the dynamics and brought it together. Tones of rich mahogany matched the fall color scheme of reds and oranges with the surrounding fabrics and throw pillows. Ryleigh's favorite colors were a deep red and burnt orange; they made her feel safe and warm inside. Her room at home was decorated in the same colors, and she loved it. Having a room decorated similar provided a little peace inside and helped to not feel so foreign.

The large picture window across the room from the doorway was surrounded by a built-in bench lined with soft pillows.

Siegfried set down Ryleigh's luggage. "Please, take your time and rest for a bit. I will be back to assist with putting away your things." He gestured toward the bed.

Ryleigh grimaced. "I'm really not that tired." Although she was exhausted, she didn't want anyone telling her that she needed to take a nap. She wasn't a two-year-old.

Siegfried held his hand to stop her from speaking any further, "Miss Vera says you need to rest, I suggest you heed her commands."

Ryleigh was a little taken aback. Siegfried left and pulled the door behind him. She heard a latch close and stood there for a moment before walking to the door.

Locked.

Anger welled from the pit of her stomach, and she pulled on the door handle. Ryleigh felt like calling out and screaming to be let out that instant but stopped herself. Instead, she stood still attempting to absorb the moment. It was then that she thought she felt something in the room with her. The air surrounding her felt electric. She noticed the hairs on her arms standing on end.

Turning around, she closed her eyes not wanting to face what might be there. Her breathing came sharp and fast, and she started to feel as if she were going to be sick. Heart beating nearly through her chest, she slowly started to open her eyes. Nothing. There was nothing there. She could feel as if something was standing right in front of her. Hesitantly, she reached out her hand and felt nothing but air.

She shook her head, scolding herself for being so silly as she walked to the bed. Throwing herself back into the mattress, she stared at the canopy admiring the pattern of leaves above her looking like autumn foliage. It was strangely comforting. She closed her eyes, taking a deep breath while trying to clear her head of all that had happened in the past few days. An overwhelming sense of sadness resonated from her chest and threatened to flow from her eyes, but she shook it away.

There was something that she was missing: an aunt arriving out of nowhere, a new place to live, surviving a wreck that decimated her parents, and now things strange and unusual happening to her. She closed her eyes. She needed to think about everything that was happening and try to gain control over her emotions. It was only a few hours since she left the hospital, and she was already imprisoned in a person's house that she did not know or understand. An aunt. Family. At least she had that someone, for now.

She closed her eyes and drifted to sleep.

* * *

Siegfried ventured downstairs to report back to Vera. He thought about how remarkable it was that Ryleigh looked just like her father. Siegfried had served the Simmons family for generations. This generation, however, was a little surprising. The children had come few and far -between over the last few years; and so far, Ryleigh was the only child that had been around in the past thirty years. None of the other members of the family reported having children. Vera was not happy about that at all. Their children were their greatest asset. It was how they carried on their power. Or, extracted it. Vera needed Ryleigh. She needed her very much.

Siegfried reported back to Vera, interrupting her thoughts. "Madam, she is in her room and secured."

Vera was extremely pleased with how things were progressing. "Very well, you are dismissed."

Siegfried turned and walked toward away, relieved that his day was over for the moment. He retired to the quietness of his room.

Vera entered her study off the main foyer. Her office was lavishly decorated in the most expensive décor money could buy. It was classy and chic. Nothing but the best. Mahogany was the preferred choice of the wood in the house; it was her favorite and was cleansed easily.

Vera contemplated her next move. She knew that family would start coming out of the woodwork. Picking up the phone, she dialed an all too familiar number, "Yes, Fin, I have her." The only words that she spoke before hanging up the phone.

Vera didn't understand why she felt so nervous. She had been preparing for this moment for the past few weeks. Ever since she'd received word that Tom and Adrianne had a child, she knew this day would come. Calling Finar was a necessary evil.

* * *

Pressing a button on the intercom, she called Siegfried back into her office once more before dismissing him for the evening. "Fin is coming," she said with a nervous laugh.

Siegfried understood what this meant. "Yes, madam, I will prepare his rooms and call in the staff." The staff. The only time that she employed more than Siegfried, who'd been with her since she herself was a child, was when individuals like Finar came calling.

Siegfried knew the only thing that Vera would ever fear was Finar and his wrath. Finding the child gave Vera an edge that none of the others had or will have. The Elders would want a peek at Ryleigh – the blessed child from a blasphemous marriage.

Vera gave Siegfried a look as if she knew what he was thinking, "I know you are worried about what Ryleigh is, but let me guarantee you that I will have her under control before anyone has time to convince her to be on their side. That includes Tristan and Illeana. I've smelled them meddling in my affairs, and I will have none of it." Siegfried nodded in understanding, "They need to know that I am in charge, and that I am the one who gets prime rights for this child. I am her guardian, after all," Vera commented.

"Yes, ma'am." Siegfried turned to make preparations for Finar. He would not be happy. Not happy at all that the child had been found. Now would be the time for a serious power struggle.

"Siegfried," Vera called after him. "Yes, Miss?"

"Please bring Ryleigh downstairs for dinner."

"Yes, Miss," Siegfried answered, knowing that this would be the last normal dinner Ryleigh would ever have in her life.

5

Time for a new family

Ryleigh was awake when Siegfried unlocked the door. The long shadows cast on the walls let her know a few hours had passed while she was sleeping. After she awoke, she found the bathroom connected to her room and was grateful for the familiarity the hot water cascading along her skin provided.

After her shower, she had waited patiently for the door to open. She wanted answers and would even be willing to wait for them, but for an aunt to be excited to see her and then lock her in her room, that was a bit bizarre. The urge to yell, kick, and scream was tempting, and Ryleigh could feel *something* slightly familiar growing in the pit of her stomach – a gnawing and urgent sensation beginning to rub her insides raw that set her nerves on edge.

Siegfried walked into the room with an air of someone other than a butler. "Miss Vera requests you downstairs."

This is what Ryleigh was waiting for. She was waiting for a moment to approach her aunt and get some answers to her long awaited questions. As Ryleigh shuffled past Siegfried, she extended her hand to brush his arm and thank him for attempting to show her a bit of kindness.

Siegfried jumped back as if she stung him. "Do not ever touch me, madam. Ever," he said with disgust resonating from his timbre.

Ryleigh's jaw dropped in confusion. Stammering an apology, she continued out the door and down the hall to the foyer where she met her Aunt Vera.

Upon seeing Ryleigh, her face broke into a genuine smile. Her long blonde hair was down and looked as if she had walked out of a salon with each strand intentionally placed for a dramatic effect. She'd changed into a trendy pair of jeans, cream colored blouse, and topped the look with red stilettos. She opened her arms wide inviting her in for an embrace.

"Ryleigh, how are you feeling? Come here and give your aunt a proper greeting."

Ryleigh needed the affection. The pain she felt was minimal compared to the comfort she needed at that moment. Once she started hugging her, she couldn't let go. She didn't want to. She needed to collapse into another human being. She needed to feel needed and loved, and in that one moment, she needed to comprehend all of what had happened to her.

Ryleigh fell to the ground and began to sob – controlled and quiet. Vera followed her to the floor. As the tears began to flow more freely, the intensity increased and her body began to shake. Vera clutched Ryleigh tighter and continued to hold her wracking body until she was done. Wiping her face with the arm of her sleeve Ryleigh sputtered between sobs, "Thank you, for everything."

Vera waved her hand toward Siegfried and uttered, "Tissues." They were in her hands immediately.

Ryleigh leaned into her aunt's chest. She rested her head against Vera's right shoulder, allowing herself to be held by this woman she didn't even know and wasn't even sure that she was related to.

"Come, come, my darling," Vera comforted, pulling her up from the ground and leading her into the formal dining area. It was an extremely large room. The table that centered the room seated at least thirty people. Dark wood with golden vines trailing along the sides and legs of the tables matched the chairs. Each chair was ornate in its own right. The fabric sparkled with tinted gold and deep chocolate brown patterns that reminded Ryleigh of autumn once more. The candelabra adorning the center of the table matched the etchings and were also gold with dark brown candles burning. Two places were set toward the head of the table. One at the exact head and one to the right.

Vera took her place at the head and motioned Ryleigh to the other seat. Siegfried pulled and pushed her chair in and then repeated the motions for Ryleigh. She sat as Siegfried pushed her chair in for her a little unsure as this was foreign to her. She hadn't had anyone ever pull out a chair for her in her life.

Ryleigh was still continuing to compose herself after her outburst. "Aunt…Vera?"

"Yes, my darling," Vera replied giving Ryleigh room to speak. Vera was prepared to answer all of Ryleigh's questions, but she kept thinking about needing to prepare for Finar's arrival and Ryleigh's emergence.

"I am not quite sure what is going on here. I am just trying to deal with…" Ryleigh choked on her words for a moment, trying to explain to her Aunt Vera the confusion she was feeling. Being in the hospital for a few weeks and then finding out she has family that she never knew about. "…my mother and my father dying, the accident…you. I am not quite sure what is going on here."

Vera grabbed Ryleigh's hand, squeezing it, and looking at her square in the eyes. She had so many things that she wanted to say but could only allow so much information to break through the dam she'd held onto for seventeen years. "Ryleigh, I am your family now. Your dad and I didn't get along for many years; however, he still loved me enough to assign me as your guardian should anything ever have happened to him or to your mother." Vera paused watching Ryleigh's face. At the mention of her parents, Ryleigh forced her eyes shut in an attempt to whisk away the tears that threatened to flow once more. "I want you to know that I have your best interest in mind. We should try and keep things as normal as possible. And by that, I mean school. Friends. There are also some things that we need to discuss that can wait until a later time, but for now, let's get you strong and back into good health again."

Ryleigh offered a small smile to acknowledge how grateful she was. All Ryleigh wanted to do was to go back into her room and cry but she knew that she also needed to eat and…she needed to run. She needed to get rid of the gnawing sensation growing in the pit of her stomach with sweat and strength as her father taught her.

The smell of food caught her attention. Her rumbling stomach started giving her fits, and she realized exactly how hungry she was. All of a sudden, people –servants – appeared, bringing trays of food and setting plates in front of her and her aunt.

Ryleigh's mouth started watering. "Wow, everything smells so good."

Vera smiled, "I'm glad. It's nothing special. I figured you would need ample sustenance."

Ryleigh replied with a slight grin, "I don't think I've ever seen this much food in one setting before." Ryleigh stopped for a moment before reaching for the food in front of her. Looking at Vera, she asked, "Would you mind…terribly…if maybe we said some kind of…something? For my mom and dad."

Vera's face went blank and then softened. "Yes," Vera cleared her throat, "we could do that."

Ryleigh grabbed Vera's hand and closed her eyes, hoping her parents were in a happier place. She wasn't quite sure what to do or say; only that she hoped there was something beyond…this.

"I am sure that your mom and dad would have appreciated that."

Ryleigh smiled at her Aunt Vera and her voracious appetite kicked in. She consumed her meal as if she hadn't eaten in weeks.

Vera chuckled, "Slow down, dear, trust me; this is not going to go anywhere."

Ryleigh grinned and took another bite of. "It's delicious. I am so hungry right now I could eat an entire cow. The hospital food left something to be desired."

Vera laughed and they continued to enjoy their first meal together.

After dinner, Vera took Ryleigh into the drawing room. A roaring fire cast light into the darkness. The drawing room was also as ornately decorated as the rest of the house. Ryleigh was not surprised by this as every room that she entered followed the same extravagant pattern and color scheme.

Vera became very serious and asked Ryleigh, "What do you know about your family, my dear?" Ryleigh looked at Vera puzzled for a moment, "What do you mean?"

"I mean, what do you know about your family? Your mother, your father, your grandparents..."

Taking a deep breath, Ryleigh explained, "I don't know a whole lot. My mom and dad both said that their parents were dead, and they were only children, which is what got them talking and together anyway…the amount of things they had in common. Because I was the only child, not that they didn't try for more, we did a lot as a family. I didn't really have a whole lot of friends growing up because we moved around a lot, but we were very close." Ryleigh could feel the sobs threatening to come back up her throat and she swallowed – hard.

Vera nodded in understanding. "Why did you move so much?"

"Because of Dad's work. We would move for his promotions. One time we moved from Texas to Canada. That was an adjustment." Ryleigh laughed at the memories that came flooding back from that move. Her dad started saying "eh" a lot during the transition and bought skis so they could learn "how-to" as a family.

Vera then asked, "Did you know that you have grandparents on both sides, and your mother has a brother. And…" Vera hesitated, "…you have an uncle."

Ryleigh looked up from her finger playing. "I have an uncle?"

"Yes, and he will be here tomorrow," Vera said self-assuredly. "His name is Finar, Fin as he likes to be called, and he will be arriving early in the morning. We are to prepare for his visit. He is your mother's brother."

"Okay?"

"By prepare, I mean, we need to ensure we are up early and ready for his arrival. He is a little more "old school" and expects things to be done a certain way. So, we shall do them the way he expects. And now, it is late, you need sleep."

Ryleigh hadn't been told to go to bed at a certain time since she was ten years old. To hear it again was foreign, but this wasn't her home yet. Not really. "Yes, of course, I am tired. But, um, Aunt Vera?"

"Yes, darling?"

"Could you *not* lock my door anymore? I didn't think I was a prisoner here. Also, I like would like to start running again as soon as I am able. Is it possible to get more information about trails around here?"

Vera was stunned by how forward Ryleigh was. She'd half expected her to be as meek as her own brother. "Yes, of course. Siegfried will provide you with information on the local hiking – running trails. Also, locking your door was never meant as an action to keep you prisoner. I only wanted to protect you from waking in an environment you are unfamiliar with. I wouldn't want you stumbling about and getting hurt in unknown territory."

Ryleigh was relieved. Had Vera answered otherwise, Ryleigh wasn't quite sure what she would have said next.

"Good night, Aunt Vera," Ryleigh reached over for a hug. She needed the embrace. She needed the contact in order to get her through the night. She needed to know there was someone that cared for her. Because inside, she felt utterly alone.

6

And now for another introduction

Morning came quickly to Ryleigh after a full stomach. Dreams about her parents plagued her through the night. Moments of seeing them alive and then…dead. Reaching out to her. She'd woken up more than once with tears streaming from her eyes.

She could also remember a dream about a boy. A boy with the whitest white of hair that imbued her with a sense of calm. A sense of clarity. She didn't know who he was, but she was eager to dream about him again. She wanted to go back to sleep to continue dreaming of him; however, she remembered her Aunt Vera's warning about being up early for her Uncle Fin.

She woke up at about 5:30 a.m. in order to hit the ground running…or rather – walking. She was still in recovery and knew her body was not ready for the physical rigor she would normally put it through. She tested her door handle and it was unlocked as requested. There was also a note pinned to her door with a map of the closest hiking trail. The sun was starting to rise which rendered the outside desert in perfect condition: not too hot, not too cold.

She stretched out the best she could, warmed up, and was on her way. The desert never ceased to amaze her. New Mexico was by far her favorite place on earth. She loved the way the sun created the ultimate canvas with its array of colors. Ryleigh was not an artist, but she could appreciate it just the same. She loved nature. She could almost hear the desert humming in her ears providing music to her soul. The familiar smell of the morning greeted her nostrils as her feet pressed her forward. Because it had been a few weeks for her to experience physical activity, she felt that first sheen of sweat cover her skin within moments. The familiarity of being healthy and in control provided her an internal peace. She yearned for that feeling. It was almost like an addictive drug. Her skin craved the sweat that she would create. Her lungs seemed to wait for the burn.

She followed the map that Siegfried made for her and started thinking about the events that brought her here. It had been only a few weeks since the accident. The police were unable to recover her parents' bodies from the crash – all she would have to visit at the cemetery were headstones dedicated to her "loving parents."

At the reading of the will, control of her parent's estate, which was meager, and guardianship was passed to Aunt Vera. She thought about how surprising it was that she had all these relatives, and her parents never once discussed it with her. She wondered why and hoped for answers.

Her body started to protest against the minimal exercise. She could feel that she was pushing it too far. She slowed down her walk, listening to her body. Her dad always told her to listen to her body and watch for the signs it was giving her. Thinking about her dad drew sadness from her chest. She pushed it back down, compartmentalizing it, refusing to allow it to surface. She needed to move forward and think about the future. She knew that is what her parents would want her to do.

She needed to listen to her body, and right now it was telling her to turn around and go back or she would regret it. She decided to listen this time. But next time she would push it a little further.

By the time she got back to the house, an hour and a half had passed. The sun rose to greet the morning, casting its rays, shedding light into the once-hidden shadowy crevices. Ryleigh took a moment to appreciate her aunt's mansion in this morning light. The sun brought out the reflective specks in the bricks surrounding the home that made it look as if they were made of gold.

Siegfried was there to greet her upon her return. "I trust you found your way around?"

"I did. I appreciated the map. I'm back earlier than I anticipated. I am just not ready to push it."

Siegfried offered her a slight smile. "Breakfast will be served shortly."

"Thank you," Ryleigh replied and ran up the stairs to her room to take a shower.

She emerged to the glorious smell of bacon. Although the home was large, the smell of bacon made a beeline path to Ryleigh's nose. She wanted to head downstairs but decided to check her email. She'd sent Cy an email. She missed him terribly. It was hard not to see him every day. He promised he would write her, video chat, keep in touch – they didn't live too far and by bus – it was only two hours. They'd both promised to get together as soon as Ryleigh was well enough.

She logged into her messenger services and responded to a few messages from her other gaming friends before logging back off. She hadn't received anything back from Cy and was disappointed…once again. She wasn't sure why he wasn't talking to her and decided that she was going to give him a call before the day was over.

Heading down the stairway, a foreign male voice echoed toward her. She entered the dining room and paused looking at a man who was a male replication of her mother. Tall, thin, handsome. He was much taller than her mother, over six feet at least, and his nose curved under slightly like a bird's beak. His dark chocolate eyes glinted as he extended his hand in a formal greeting.

"…and you must be Ryleigh. I am your Uncle Fin and I am *very* glad to meet you."

Ryleigh grabbed his hand as he offered it to her and Vera cleared her throat. "Breakfast is ready and we do not want it cold," she said snidely.

Fin turned and gave Vera a knowing glance, "Yes, you are right. We must eat. I am famished."

Fin laughed as he turned toward the dining room. He immediately took a seat at the head of the table. Vera stood by the chair with a look of surprise on her face. How dare this man enter her home and take over! But, it was the way of things. It was how it was done, and she would not argue. Instead, she took a breath, and sat directly across from Ryleigh.

Siegfried entered the dining area with the staff from last night that seemed to appear out of thin air. The aromas were mouthwatering, and Ryleigh imagined she would need to wipe drool from her chin.

"Everything smells amazing!" Ryleigh complimented.

"Yes, it does," admired Fin. "Your Aunt Vera has to make sure that everything is perfect, including the eggs that are served in this household." Taking a bite of bacon, "Right, love?" he asked.

"Yes," agreed Vera. "Perfect." Although she appeared to smile, her eyes conveyed a deeper message that only Fin could understand.

Breakfast proceeded as normal, and after the dishes were cleared, the new family retired to the living room. Ryleigh wondered who this uncle was that would now seem to be a part of her new life.

Fin stared at Ryleigh, thinking how much she resembled his sister, her mother. Drawing breath, he apologized, "Ryleigh, I am so sorry that until now we have had no contact. But…your mother and father wanted it that way. They wanted no part of this kind of life." Fin gestured towards the house.

Ryleigh was confused. Why would her parents not want this kind of lifestyle? She thought maybe they wanted to make it on their own. Her dad was a contractor and her mom stayed at home – she thought they did pretty well.

Interrupting her thoughts Fin said, "I know you must be wondering what is going on, and why I am here…" he drew closer to her, placing his hand on her knee, "…but, I must reassure you that we want nothing but the best for you."

Ryleigh's heart started to race and she felt a little more than uncomfortable. A pulling sensation emanated from the where Fin placed his hand. She looked at her aunt who was sitting across from her calmly and started to panic. Ryleigh grabbed Fin's hand.

"Fin!" Vera barked.

Fin removed his hand and Ryleigh started to breathe a little more easily.

"Please, please excuse me," Ryleigh said, standing up from the couch. She felt as if she were going to lose the breakfast she just consumed. Barely making it to the bathroom on time, she wretched violently. Ryleigh thought her internal organs were going to come lose.

Vera called to her gently from behind the door, "Ryleigh, are you okay?"

Ryleigh leaned her forehead onto the seat of the cool porcelain toilet knowing that it was clean enough to eat your lunch from. "Yeah, I'll be okay. Just, uh, give me a minute. I think I overdid it this morning." But even as the words spilled from her mouth, she knew it wasn't true. She knew that there was something more in the works here. And she was going to find out what it was exactly.

* * *

After Ryleigh's vomiting episode, Fin and her aunt vanished into the study that doubled as Vera's office. Returning to the living room, Ryleigh stared out the large picture window at the scenic landscape. Had the accident not happened, she would be home hanging out with Cy – who she needed to call, desperately. With Vera's home separated from the surrounding community, there didn't seem to be anyone her age for her to connect with. Ryleigh wasn't sure what the rules and limits were without incurring the wrath of Siegfried. She had a feeling he didn't like her.

Voices rose from behind the dark heavy door. The deep baritone of her uncle resonated through the wood. Vera's quiet undertones barely audible. This was her new family. *Family.* More than her parents. What a strange concept.

She'd always been jealous of other kids growing up. Around the holidays, birthdays, and other gatherings, she would wonder what it would or could be like to have family other than just her parents. Now that these relatives had found her, she didn't know how to feel. Betrayed? Did her parents betray her? How could they have segregated themselves from their own blood? Having craved family her entire childhood – grandparents, cousins, aunts, uncles – Ryleigh was disappointed. She felt guilty for allowing these feelings to surface. How could they have excluded this side of family from her? She'd always felt so lonely. And now, she wouldn't have to. Would she?

Interrupting her thoughts, the door to the study opened abruptly and Fin stormed out. "You mind what I said, Vera. You mind it, or you will be on the other side."

Vera watched him walk out the front door. She brushed her hands down the front of her jeans and Ryleigh could see her face that was, just moments ago darkened with anger, soften as she walked towards Ryleigh.

"What was that about?" Ryleigh asked.

"Nothing, really. It's your uncle, being your uncle," her aunt said unconvincingly.

"Is it about me?" Ryleigh had an overwhelming sense that it was.

Vera raised a perfectly waxed eyebrow. "No. It's not," she said unconvincingly. "Even if it were, it wouldn't be anything for you to worry about. At least – not right now." And with that ominous ending, Vera turned and walked out of the room.

7

New year, new school

Before Ryleigh knew it, time blinked away. The days became cooler, turning the season to fall, which meant starting a new school. Again. Ryleigh was not looking forward to starting another new year – her senior year at that.

Although she didn't have many friends at her old school, she'd looked forward to knowing the same people as before. This school year would be even harder for her. The social niches and cliques that had been formed since freshman year didn't have room for any outsiders. She expected to end the school year as she would begin it. New. Unknown. Unbelonging.

Ryleigh spent hours attempting to convince her aunt to allow her to be homeschooled for this final year; however, Vera felt it necessary for Ryleigh to integrate herself into the teenage social order. Ryleigh needed to "socialize" herself. She'd spent hours on the computer: gaming, chatting, and reading instead of interacting with real people.

Ryleigh was not happy. And even visibly not so. This was her last year, a new home, a new family…what choice did she have?

Walking into San Andreas High brought back old anxieties. Ryleigh tried to push those aside as she looked for the office to get her schedule. Her Aunt Vera took it upon herself to register Ryleigh without her, so she didn't get an opportunity to discuss her class schedule with the counselor. She was ahead in credits and planned on graduating early; however, every school was different.

It didn't matter which school she went to, they all smelled the same, they had the same kids, the same cliques…the layout might be different, but overall it was the same. She just had to remind herself of this. And, the silver lining, she could always call Cy during lunch. He'd finally gotten back in touch with her. She was relieved to have him back in her life. It was weird without him. Having the distance separated them. Even having a status of "best friend" couldn't make up for the miles between them.

The office was immediately to her right when walking through the front doors. It smelled of coffee and toner intertwined with cologne and perfume. The combination made Ryleigh nauseous, but it was tolerable.

A few kids were standing in front of her in the line. Ryleigh glanced around the office, waiting her turn, and felt a shove in her back. She flipped around shouting, "Hey!" but nothing was there. Great, now she was going to look crazy. At least fifteen students were milling around the office. For one moment, it seemed as if they were all looking at her like she might be crazy. *Yep, that was Ryleigh, crazy girl.* Let the rumors generate now... Ryleigh turned back around and there was one person left in front of her at the counter. She felt someone shove her again as she stumbled and turned around to find nothing there…yet again. She knew she wasn't imagining it, and told herself that if it happened again, she was just going to ignore it.

Except… it happened again. This time, she stumbled directly into the blonde guy in front of her. Who, in turn, belly flopped onto the counter.

"Oh…crap," Ryleigh said, turning red from her own embarrassment. "I-I am so sorry, I wasn't paying attention…" Her voice trailed off as the blonde turned around rubbing his stomach.

Ryleigh hadn't ever had an immediate crush just looking at some guy, but this one, she could see herself drooling over.

"It's okay," he said. Even his voice was covered in honey and sticky sweet, something she could imagine listening to.

Composing herself, she smiled and introduced herself. "I'm Ryleigh. And…I really am sorry for that."

He grinned back, flashing a perfect smile and white teeth. She could almost smell the mint of his breath. "It's okay. Really. I'm Tristan." The secretary he was speaking with called his name and he turned back around.

I could get used to this school, she thought as he left the office. He offered a wink as they passed each other. She watched him walk out the door, admiring him from the back. Hearing a throat clearing, she turned back around.

"And how can I help you?" asked the secretary.

"My Aunt Vera registered me, and I need to pick up my schedule," Ryleigh said.

She gave her name and was pointed toward the guidance counselor's office where she was made to wait again. She could see that this day was going to drag by slowly. After a ten minute wait, Ryleigh was called into the office.

A gentle looking man stood behind the desk and smiled as Ryleigh entered the small personal office. She could smell printer paper and peppermint, not an unpleasant combination. The man introduced himself as Mr. Mauer.

They reviewed her credits and put her schedule together for the first semester. Ryleigh was pleased that she would still have the opportunity to graduate early.

Leaving the office with schedule in hand, she was given directions to her first class of the day. Since she'd already missed homeroom, her class would be history –something she detested. She loved to watch documentaries about the past, but sitting in a classroom reading chapters and reciting passages was extremely boring. Ryleigh learned when it was fun. Not when it was painfully dry.

Entering the classroom late was always an experience. All heads turn when the door opens, and she knew it would happen that way. Taking a deep breath, gathering her courage, she entered the classroom. Having the door at the rear of the class was entertaining. The definition 'rubber necking' does not quite explain the effect of twenty pairs of eyes, turning to see who entered the room. It was almost in unison; watching their heads turn as if on swivel sticks was amusing. It took everything she had not to laugh out loud.

The teacher stopped mid-sentence and smiled, "So, how can I help you?"

Ryleigh walked to the front of the classroom and handed the teacher her schedule. He glanced at it and, before pointing her to an empty chair, introduced her to the classroom. "This is Ryleigh Simmons. Ryleigh, would you like to tell us a little about yourself?"

Internally she groaned. She didn't want to talk about herself in front of these people. She could tell they weren't really interested in anything that she would have to say. So, why not just tell the truth?

"Not really," Ryleigh replied honestly.

"Okay then," Mr. Ray drawled and invited her to her newly assigned seat. She saw Tristan sitting comfortably on the other side of the classroom - staring at her. She glanced his way and sat down trying not to cause too much of a disturbance, knowing that she was the "new girl."

The rest of the morning progressed. Ryleigh did get lost a few times trying to find the classrooms she belonged to and had to force herself to ask for directions.

Lunch crept up like a cat waiting to pounce. This was what she was afraid of, the moment when she would have to find a place to sit down and eat, and socialize, and interact. It wasn't as if there were kids throwing themselves at her feet. She hadn't met anyone that suited her personality, or anyone that showed an interest in getting to know her…yet.

Ryleigh scoped out the lunchroom as she made her way through the line. She didn't bring her lunch today. Her aunt gave her money to choose something a la carte. It didn't matter what school she was in. The food was all the same. Disgusting.

She didn't like vegetables and avoided them at all cost. It didn't matter if it was at home or at school, if there were vegetables, she would not eat them. She grimaced at the vegetarian menu the school had. She couldn't understand how anyone could consume something named "bean curd" and looked like sewage. It boggled her mind. Instead, she chose a hamburger, fries – the only vegetable she would eat – and a soft drink.

She paid for her meal and surveyed the room. Suddenly, she could feel someone standing next to her. Turning her head, she sighed, it was Tristan.

"Need some place to sit?" he asked nonchalantly.

Ryleigh, ever the one for sarcasm, said, "No, I think I would just rather stand here and eat my lunch."

Tristan laughed, "Come on."

Ryleigh stood there for a minute just wondering what the catch could possibly be. He turned around and motioned for her to follow him. Instead, she walked the opposite direction. She didn't feel like being friendly and didn't feel like being made fun of. She didn't look back, but she could feel his gaze on her back. And for the first time, she didn't feel self-conscious about it. Which was weird…even for her.

* * *

The school day continued to progress normally; but, by the end of the day, Ryleigh could feel the tension building in her body. She felt on edge. She didn't have problems with anyone, but she could feel the stress. Somehow, some students were aware of her parent's death and gave their condolences. Offering a fake grin and saying "thank you" was a little too much for her to bear when she didn't even care about these people.

After school, Siegfried was waiting for her in the car. If she could even seem even more like a rich kid dork, this was it as plain as day. She rolled her eyes at Siegfried when she got into the car. "Really," she questioned. "Right out front?"

"Yes, Miss Ryleigh, it is as your aunt instructed." As Siegfried pulled away from the school, she saw Tristan looking at the car intently.

Siegfried stared at her in the rear view mirror, "Did you make any friends today?"

"Um, not really," Ryleigh responded, jamming her headphones into her ears not offering a further response. The ride continued as she listened to her music and stared blankly out the vehicle's tinted windows.

They pulled up to the house in no time. The view still amazed her every time she saw it. The fact that she still lived in this house amazed her every single time.

She noticed a few cars out front but didn't think anything of it. Her aunt always had visitors at the house. However, as she looked at the cars, she noticed a trend. Each car had a unique sigil or symbol. It was the same one she discovered on what she assumed was her family crest. The symbol resembled an ankh with a tail. It drew her in, and yet, at the same time, repulsed her. She wasn't sure why, and she hadn't asked her aunt about it. It was on her ever-growing list of things to do. She still needed to have a conversation with her aunt about her family, but there was always something that came up.

Ryleigh entered the house expecting to immediately go upstairs to become invisible until dinner, but Siegfried stopped her, "Miss Vera wants to see you in the study."

Ryleigh was a little surprised as she rarely saw her aunt until the evenings. "Really? You couldn't tell me this prior to walking in the door?" She was annoyed. Siegfried took her things and Ryleigh entered the study.

The study was more like a library. Each wall had built-in bookshelves from floor to ceiling. The décor continued the theme of the house – dark wood, inlaid with gold trimming. The smell of old books, paper, and scented candles gave Ryleigh a sense of comfort.

"Come in, darling, there are some people that you need to meet," Vera said, opening her arms for an embrace.

Hugging her aunt, she noticed three separate couples sitting around the room. What stood out to her is that their faces seemed similar in appearance – the only differences were their ages. Vera, behind her desk, motioned for Ryleigh to take a place on the settee just to her left, facing these strange people.

"These are also members of our family," Vera started pointing them out as she stood up from her desk and walked behind each person. "These are your grandparents, my mother and father," she said with a smile, flashing her pearly whites at Ryleigh. As Vera introduced each adult, she touched them briefly on the shoulder. Ryleigh smiled and said hello.

"These are your mother and Fin's grandparents," Vera pointed out. Again Ryleigh offered another "hello" and faint smile not knowing how to respond. She decided to wait until the introductions were complete.

"And this lovely couple," Vera said, touching both of them at the same time, "are your cousins." Ryleigh noticed they stiffened a little when Vera placed her hands on their shoulders. "They also have children that you will be meeting shortly. They go to the same school as you do."

Ryleigh stared at this beautiful group of people. Although they had the same facial characteristics, she noticed the differences between each of them. Either pair of "grandparents" looked similar and yet different. It was as if they were a plastic image of what a grandparent were supposed to look like. The lines and wrinkles were apparent. However; their eyes looked much older than the image their body projected. There was a cold hardness to the way they stared at her, although their facial expression suggested that they were happy to meet her.

Vera motioned Ryleigh over to her relatives for formal introductions when the door to the study opened. As she glanced at the door, she stopped mid-track.

"The children are here," Siegfried said. As he stepped away, two shadows emerged from behind him.

The first person who entered the study was a girl about Ryleigh's age. The first thing Ryleigh noticed about her was her long hair, white as fresh winter snow. She had high cheek bones, a small upturned nose, and violet eyes. She was beautiful and gracious. As she moved in the room, her clothes flowed with her walk. It was as if an invisible breeze encased every movement, allowing the wispy fabric to participate in each step. Her clothing was lightly colored and matched the radiance that emanated from beneath her skin.

"This is Illeana," Vera said gesturing to the girl. "And this…is Tristan." Tristan emerged from behind Illeana. Ryleigh sucked in her breath sharply.

Vera glanced at Ryleigh seeing the recognition in her eyes. "Ah," Vera commented. "I see that you two have met then have you?"

Ryleigh nodded," Yes, we met today and have some classes together."

"Well then, come greet your family properly," Vera encouraged.

Ryleigh greeted each family member as if it were a wedding or funeral line – trying to shake or at least grip each person's hand in welcome. Or rather, they would grab hers and hold on for a second. By the time she got to the end of the line, she felt sapped of energy, and her hand was warm and sweaty.

When she approached Illeana, Illeana placed both hands on Ryleigh's shoulders, "Greetings, cousin, I certainly hope to get to know you much better."

Ryleigh stared into Illeana's eyes, marveling at how translucent and yet dense they seemed at the same time, entranced with their violet luminescence. Ryleigh nodded automatically and snapped back to reality when Illeana broke the physical connection.

Tristan placed his hands on Ryleigh's shoulders as she stood in front of him, "Greetings cousin," he said. Ryleigh felt a little uncomfortable and embarrassed. "I am glad to meet you," he continued.

"Did you know who I was before?" Ryleigh asked, curious to see if she would get an honest answer.

"Yes, I knew who you were. But, it was not my place to say anything at the time."

Vera cleared her throat. Ryleigh didn't realize he still had his hands on her shoulders until he removed them.

Ryleigh's face felt flush and dizzy. Beads of perspiration broke across her forehead. "Aunt Vera," she started. "I think I am going to go change and take a shower. It's been a long first day."

Vera nodded, "Come down when you are finished. Everyone is staying for dinner."

Ryleigh left the study. Half way up the stairs she heard the study door open behind her.

"Wait," she heard Tristan say.

She stopped, thinking that she owed Tristan an apology for earlier. "Look, I'm sorry about earlier. I'm not normally that rude but…it was the first day and –"

Tristan interrupted her. "It's fine," he said. "However, I do need to talk to you…but not here."

Ryleigh cocked her head to the side, wondering what this new cousin could possibly have to talk to her about. Tristan gazed back with his piercing blue eyes. Ryleigh found herself thinking about Tristan in a way that one should never think of a cousin and immediately shut those thoughts down.

"Um, okay," Ryleigh said. She was unused to all this newness. It was hard enough to adjust to this new life, but now adjusting to a new family, it was all happening too quickly.

"Okay, when do you want to talk," Ryleigh finally decided – curious.

Tristan drew closer to Ryleigh, leaning into her, whispering in her ear with hot breath standing the hairs on her body to attention. "We'll talk tomorrow at lunch," he promised. Tristan turned abruptly and walked back to the study.

Ryleigh shook her head, gathering her senses. What was wrong with her?

* * *

Dinner went by without a hitch. It was politeness with an edge of nervousness thrown in. Ryleigh chose not to stick around after dinner and instead retreated to her room. She jumped on the computer to see if Cy was online. He never was anymore and that hurt. It was severely disappointing. Even though she had only known him for a year, he was the only friend that she'd actually kept over the years and made an attempt to stay in touch with. Prior to falling asleep that evening, Ryleigh replayed the afternoon's scene with Tristan over and over. Ryleigh wasn't sure what he needed to tell her, but she knew it couldn't be good.

8

All those dirty little secrets

School the next day was the same as the previous with one exception, Ryleigh wasn't as nervous. Tristan was in her homeroom as well as her History class. She offered him a hello from across the room. The morning passed, and before Ryleigh knew it, it was lunch. She meandered through the line picking a hamburger, no bread, and a soft drink.

Ryleigh had woken up with her stomach complaining. She was ravenous. For breakfast, she downed four eggs, eight pieces of bacon, orange juice, six sausage links, and two glasses of milk. She attributed it to starting her running regimen and going to school. She decided to take it easy on lunch, although she felt she could eat an entire cow and its calves.

She saw Tristan waving at her from across the room, motioning for her to come to his table. This time she didn't walk away.

Walking over to the table, she passed by the usual conglomeration of cliques. The gorgeous, the geeky, the inept, the socially awkward, the artistic, *et cetera*… She wouldn't have anything to do with any club or group. Ryleigh was comfortable being herself and didn't feel as if she needed to project any outward façade to incorporate into any group or clique within the social order of high school. Today, she wore her favorite pair of dark blue jeans; band t-shirt, and black combat boots. Regardless of where anyone thought she "belonged", she never gave into the stereotype. She dressed and did things her way.

"Glad you decided to sit with me today," Tristan remarked with his winning smile.

"Yeah, well, you said you had something to tell me," Ryleigh replied, hoping this wouldn't take too much time so she could eat and get out of there.

"I am not going to tell you here." Tristan motioned around the cafeteria. "Eat your lunch and then we'll go." Ryleigh looked at Tristan as if he were nuts.

"What do you mean go?" Ryleigh asked.

"Off campus."

"I am not skipping school," Ryleigh replied adamantly. "I have plans to graduate early, and there is no way I am jeopardizing that by cutting class."

Tristan leaned in across the table. "You need to know what happened to your mom and dad. You need to know who you are."

Ryleigh stilled. She was as a stone gargoyle forever guarding a chapel. Swallowing her pride and realizing the information could be more important than an early graduation date, she agreed. "Fine," she said. "I'm done now. Let's go."

Ryleigh grabbed her tray as she stood up and walked to dump it in the garbage. She turned expecting to see Tristan behind her, but he was still sitting at the table. "Are you coming or what?" she asked as she continued out the cafeteria. Tristan, a little surprised, followed suit.

Ryleigh waited for him outside the cafeteria doors. "So, *where* are we going and *how* are we getting there?" Ryleigh asked impatiently.

"We are getting away from this school and from prying ears," Tristan said.

How aggravating. Ryleigh wanted answers. Now would be her chance to finally get them.

The pair walked off the school campus and into the surrounding neighborhood. Ryleigh followed Tristan until he stopped beside a golden toned mini Cooper. He pushed the button on his key ring disabling the alarm and unlocking the doors, "Hop in."

Ryleigh was hesitant. She hardly knew Tristan, even if he was family, but she had an internal whisper that said he wouldn't harm her, that it would be okay. She knew that no harm would come to her because she trusted him. She knew in her core that she would be alright. She opened the door and got in.

* * *

Tristan jumped in and started the car. "We are going to just go for a bit of a drive. We'll be back in time for Siegfried to take you home. He will never know you left, and Aunt Vera will assume you've been in school this whole time."

"What about the automated system that says I've missed a class," Ryleigh asked, knowing that the school would call if she was marked absent or even tardy.

Tristan turned to her and smiled. "Don't worry about it. That system calls out randomly all the time. You could tell her it was a mistake, or, that you volunteered in another classroom and that it will be cleared up the next day. Don't sweat it."

Ryleigh shrugged. She would play it off like Tristan said as a mistake. Hopefully Vera would just accept it.

They drove for about twenty minutes into the desert. If Ryleigh wasn't sure of her instincts she would probably be panicking. Driving into the desert with someone she hardly knew was the perfect scene for stupid-girl-gets-murdered. Tristan pulled the car over, turned the engine off, and got out of the car. Ryleigh watched him for a moment. He was so sure of himself. He had an air of confidence that surrounded him. It seeped from his pores and almost drowned her.

This was so far out of Ryleigh's comfort zone. She opened the door and sat in the car for a moment. She'd only known him two days and they were already breaking rules. She laughed silently to herself. She'd wanted adventure in her life, but not this kind of adventure.

"Okay," Ryleigh questioned. "What is *so* important that we need to drive into the middle of the desert for you to tell me?" Throwing a bit of sarcasm his way, Ryleigh approached Tristan. "You don't have an axe behind you do you?"

Tristan grinned and paced backward a few steps. He turned, looking at her and taking a deep breath. As his chest rose and filled with air, Ryleigh, for just a moment, noticed a glimmer. A shift. A wave that erupted from his body and looked as if it were a mirage in the desert. She stepped back, blinking away the illusion.

"Don't be afraid," Tristan said calmly.

"What – What the heck was that?" Ryleigh asked, her heart rate continuing to increase in step with her nervousness.

"Don't freak out. But what I am going to tell you…it could be kinda scary," Tristan said very calmly.

Ryleigh swallowed, "What do you mean…scary?" Her voice started to quiver and her hands started to shake. She felt the pounding in her chest and knew that if she allowed panic to overtake her, she could react…violently.

"First of all, my parents are not my parents," Tristan remarked. "They are - something else. Something dressed to look like them."

"Wait, wait, wait a minute." Ryleigh scrunched her face in disbelief. "How are they "dressed" to look like your parents? How are they *not* your parents?"

Tristan stepped closer to Ryleigh who stepped back. "I know my own mom and dad, don't you think?" Sarcasm slowly dripped from his voice like molasses onto pancakes.

"I guess so," Ryleigh agreed. "Okay, so if they aren't your parents, then where are they?" Ryleigh just wasn't sure what to make of this talk they were having. Tristan rolled his eyes. "I don't know. I suppose they are with yours."

"You think your parents are dead?"

"No, and your parents aren't dead either."

Ryleigh suddenly felt annoyed. The words slowly rolled from her tongue, "My parents *are* dead. You are *not* funny."

Tristan stared at her. She could feel it emanating from his skin. The truth. The truth tasted bittersweet.

"They aren't dead, Ryleigh. Things are just not as they seem."

Instead of contradicting him, she wanted to know the truth. She'd felt as if things were off since leaving the hospital and moving in with Vera. "Then tell me. Tell me everything."

Tristan nodded. "I'm really not sure where to start," he began. He rifled his hands through his hair and closed his eyes for a moment. Taking a breath, he started, "Other than what Illeana and I have found out recently, I'll start at the beginning."

9

The truth, the whole truth, and nothing but the truth

"I overheard them talking," Tristan began. His gaze seemed distant despite the fact that he was staring directly into Ryleigh's eyes. "My *fake* parents or, the FPs as Illeana and I call them…"

Ryleigh nodded and tried to not let her mind wander. It was strange. Bizarre. Something unreal and unexpected. She thought for a second that maybe, just maybe, the entire family was crazy and she would make a break for it, run away, and get out of there as soon as possible.

"…they were saying something about how Tom and Adrianne were holding up nicely. They were talking to someone else on the phone, and I assumed they could have been talking about someone else, but, we figured out that it had to do with *your* mom and dad."

"When was this?" Ryleigh interrupted.

"It was about three months ago. Illeana and I just found out that you moved in with Vera. The FPs thought we were still at school, but it was half-day or something like that. We never made too much noise coming home; besides, our house is as big as yours."

"It's not really my house," Ryleigh said dismissively

"Illeana would immediately go change as soon as we got home, and I am always hungry, so I headed for the kitchen. That's when I overheard them. Normally, I wouldn't have thought anything about it, but their voices…" Tristan trailed off almost whispering. "They were different. They weren't my parents. They were… They were someone else. They didn't even know I was standing there. At first, I didn't know what to think. I didn't even know what to say as I walked by. But, I heard them. I heard them say *what* they said. And then I went upstairs and told Illeana. That's when we decided to just play along and see what happened."

Immediately, the world around Ryleigh muted, and her skull felt a tremendous pressure. She was having a hard time processing this information. That her parents were still alive after having to deal with their deaths? Missing them every hour of every day. Not after three months. That would place her moving in with Vera at the time that Tristan overheard this conversation. She couldn't breathe.

Almost gasping for breath, Ryleigh asked, "So, what do we do now? Where are my parents? Where are yours?" It was taking every ounce of control she had not to allow the tears welling in her eyes to come cascading down.

"Well, let me ask you this…what *do* you know about your parents?"

Ryleigh was puzzled by Tristan's question. What did that even mean? She only knew her parents. She had no idea about the extended family she'd recently been introduced to.

"I thought I knew my mom and dad, but you know, I didn't even know I had grandparents."

Tristan nodded and then said, "You need to talk to Vera. She needs to give you some insight into who you really are. I can't say much more than that. All I can do," Tristan said moving closer to Ryleigh, "is show you."

"Don't be afraid," he said calmly as he took another step. His voice emanated a tone that soothed her nervousness. She knew he wouldn't hurt her.

Tristan reached out to her and grabbed her hands. Ryleigh felt an electric jolt course through her hands. Her heart started to race. "Just breathe," Tristan said. "I'm going to show you what you are capable of."

Ryleigh remembered the incident with Cyrus and started to get nervous. Light began to almost seep from Tristan's skin, carving deep runic symbols; curling into purple waves of flame. As the fire spread from his arms to encase his body, it began to move from his hands to hers. Ryleigh felt a heat rising from the center of her chest. It continued to spread outward to her limbs. Ryleigh thought she could almost hear a humming, like rhythmic music, pulsing in time with the flames that rose from his body. The flame continued to creep over her hands and coat her in a purple haze.

Where the flames touched, Ryleigh felt only a gentle breeze moving along her skin. The warmth she felt from inside her own body rippled outwardly into white light. Tristan's flames began to back down as her skin started to glow. *It was surreal*, Ryleigh thought. She knew that this energy was of her own creation. She could feel the energy talking to her, almost singing to her inside of her mind with soft melodic tinkles.

Tristan looked her dead in the eyes, and she began to wonder if she could spread the light over Tristan as he had done to her. She looked down at her skin, willing it to move forward. She gasped aloud as she saw it shimmer and push toward his hands. She could feel a little resistance inside as if a barrier prevented her from moving it any further.

She pushed a little more, but this time, flames pushed her back. Ryleigh began to feel irritated. She was usually pretty good about getting things right the first time and wanted to push harder. *MOVE*, she thought, and could feel the resistance push and pull between her and Tristan. Looking up at Tristan, she noticed the confusion on his face. His eyes glinted deviously and he pushed his flames back toward her…for the last time. As he pushed back, she pushed forward and the collision of their energy blew them both apart with a force that left them sprawled in the dirt several feet away from each other and where they'd been standing.

The dust settled, and Ryleigh picked herself up from the ground. She looked across at Tristan who was doing the same, "*What* was that?"

Tristan brushed himself off and offered to help Ryleigh up. Extending his hand he replied, "We have abilities. I was seeing what you could do with yours, and what you can do…I've never seen before."

"I don't even know what that was, What I did. What did I just do?" she asked with a demure laugh.

"We have the ability to channel our energy. That is about as much as I should tell you. You need to ask your aunt the rest. And," he continued looking at his watch, "we need to get back before we are missed."

Tristan wondered if he should have told Ryleigh everything instead of leaving it to her aunt. He wanted to know what her aunt would say. He wanted to know if he could find out any more information about his parents. He wanted to know if Vera was someone they could trust.

10

Family history in the making

"Where were you today?"

That was how the night started. Apparently Aunt Vera had been keeping tabs on Ryleigh. Tabs she was quite unaware of...until now.

"I was at school," Ryleigh answered, praying she could dismiss an automated call with Tristan's excuse.

"I would rethink your answer. I know you left school today with Tristan. Where did you go?" Aunt Vera pursued.

"Why don't you tell me the truth, and I'll tell you the truth," Ryleigh challenged. She hadn't expected the answer Vera gave her and felt her privacy violated. She was seventeen, why did she need to be watched like a toddler.

"What I am going to tell you, you should have been told from the time you were able to understand words. Each child in our family is taught and instructed from the time they are born until they reach the age of seventeen. The age of *Becoming*. Faehood." Ryleigh was not prepared for the next question. "Do you know what Faerie or Fae are?"

"Um, magical creatures in children stories?" Ryleigh asked hesitantly.

"Faerie is a conglomeration of all supernatural," Vera replied.

"Supernatural," Ryleigh repeated slowly. After her experience with Tristan, she knew she wasn't normal.

"It is an all-inclusive term. Fae are every type of supernatural being you have heard or read about. Vampires. Werewolves. Demons. Witches. Fae are the keepers of the land and have existed since the beginning of the universe. Does that make sense?"

Ryleigh nodded.

"We, meaning our family, our heritage…we are descendants of the Fae." Vera waited for a response from her niece.

Ryleigh had always felt as if she were different. Under any other circumstance, she would dismiss this as crazy-talk and find a way to escape, quickly. Because of her experience with Tristan that afternoon, she knew Vera was telling the truth. That this was not crazy and she needed to know more.

Ryleigh closed her eyes and took a deep breath, "Aunt Vera, why have I never known about you or our family or any of this until now?"

"Let me tell you a little more about our history, and then I'll answer your questions," Vera responded. Ryleigh nodded as Vera continued.

"As I mentioned, Fae are supernatural. We co-existed with humanity for centuries. As humans evolved, their perceptions toward us changed. We became something to be feared because of our varying abilities. We were given negative connotations by humans and shoved into make-believe stories to sweep our kind under the rug. Fae were labeled as ones who caused death and destruction. Evil incarnate. This caused Fae to take on these personas that men gave them. We became the enemy."

Vera signaled for Siegfried to refill her tea.

"Fae often disguised themselves as human after becoming something to be feared. They lived, they loved, they had children…" Vera trailed off for a moment.

"Ryleigh. We, our family and others – as descendants, we are half-breed, partial-breed." Vera paused for a moment before asking, "Do you know what a succubus is?"

Ryleigh knew what a succubus was; she had read many stories involving the ill-fated demonic women who fed on sexual energy.

"Yes," she replied, "I do."

"Well then, you know what you are. You are Lilin." Vera crossed the room to sit in the lounger by the fire. Vera was breathtaking. Each move she made, even a twitch, seemed intentional. Vera closed her eyes, and her lashes, long and curling at the ends so perfectly, made Ryleigh secretly jealous.

"I'm not sure what you mean…exactly." Ryleigh slowly expelled with her breath. Confusion and enlightenment took over her brain. She stared at her Aunt Vera for a moment and then realized that what she was saying might be true.

"I don't get it. What do you mean I am a *Lilin*?" Ryleigh was on the verge of panic and tears. She didn't want to be anything construed as evil. She wasn't a bad person. She didn't want to be thought of that way.

Vera's British accent filled the room crisp and proper. "I've already explained to you about our Fae past." Vera became very serious. "Those of us that exist today, we are all part Fae. You, my darling, are also part Fae." Vera sat up from her chair and crossed to grab Ryleigh by the shoulders. Looking her in the eyes, she continued, "You must understand that you can never tell anyone. Nor can you have a relationship with a human. Ever."

Ryleigh sucked in her breath and started to shake her head and stammer, "B-but, that doesn't make any sense. Why now? This doesn't make any sense!"

"Because, my darling, when we turn seventeen, that is when we mature. Haven't you felt different your whole life? Known things? Seen things that weren't there that you shrugged off to your imagination? Dreamt things only to see them come true?" Ryleigh recognized some of what she experienced from Vera's talk. She nodded in agreement, "You must understand, what happened to your parents…" Vera seemed to choke back tears. She sat still for a moment composing herself before she dropped the bottom out from Ryleigh's world. "I know that your father is not dead."

Ryleigh turned and stared at Vera with disbelief. Screwing up her eyes with a little anger, "What do you mean you know my father is not dead?" Ryleigh asked more forcefully. This was twice that she had heard that father wasn't dead in one day, and she was beginning to feel nauseous.

"I know this, because your father and I are twins. We have a connection. I know he is not dead because…I can feel it. I have been looking for him and your mother since I was contacted about you, since I found you in the hospital."

"But why have I never known about you? Or anyone from our family?"

"Because your father and I had a falling out. He wanted to live as a human, and I couldn't handle that,"

Vera could remember the argument her and Tom had the day he told her that his wife was pregnant. She remembered the argument so vividly that felt as if it killed her inside.

"Although Tristan and Illeana are your cousins, I prefer you to stay away from them. They are trouble-makers and will do *nothing* but get you into trouble. Stay away from them."

Vera's eyes narrowed when mentioning Tristan and Illeana's names. Ryleigh could feel the heat emanating from Vera's skin and she started to wonder what type of Fae Vera was.

"Tomorrow, we will start training," Vera informed her as she started to walk out of the room.

"Training for what?" asked Ryleigh, realizing what she needed training for the moment the words left her lips.

"You need to learn how to control your tendencies. Fae feed on the energy of humans." Turning around she said, "You may be classified as a succubus, but that is not truly what you are. We fed false information to humans so they would not understand our kind. Our history is ensnared out there in vast amounts of misinformation." Ryleigh nodded in agreement. "There are stories out there that are slightly true; however, there are stories out there that are completely false. Succubae being one of them. You are a Chi eater and a purveyor of energy. You are Lilin."

* * *

"Witches were the first human descendants of the Fae. They worked with Fae side-by-side, helping keep order between nature and humanity, balancing black and white, good and evil. Witches were also the first to be told of the Lilin and their abilities. While each class of Fae has their own abilities, Lilin are the most powerful. All Fae have a power within them, an ebb of energy that can be used to create life, defend themselves, or even extinguish life.

This energy or life force can also be passed from one to another as an inheritance and has often happened between parent and child.

"With the good comes the bad. One the flipside of the other. It all started with one: Valen. He realized that the energy that flowed within them could not just be passed from parent to child, but could also be stolen – stolen from the young. Valen became greedy, consuming not only his own kind, but humans and Halflings, Fae/Human offspring.

"When word got out what Valen was doing, it caused ripples throughout the Fae community and a separation defining light and dark, good and evil. Before Valen's actions, there wasn't a visible line separating what was good and what was not. The Fae had always worked together in harmony, symbiotically amongst each other.

"His actions created panic and families went into hiding, fearing for themselves and for their children. Imprisoning themselves in the Sanctum. Prior to a Halfling child turning seventeen, their abilities lay dormant, unlike whole Fae whose abilities are apparent from the day they are born. Once a child reached the age of Becoming, *turning seventeen, their abilities were enabled. They came into full maturity. If not properly trained or harnessed, their power would spiral out of control killing them. Valen discovered this and his mission changed. He started to hunt seventeen-year-old Halflings. He kidnapped sixteen-year-old children, and on the child's seventeenth birthday, he would extract the Chi they carried inside them, increasing his own power, and*

killing them in the process. This made him extremely dangerous. With each extraction, he grew more powerful. The Elders attempted to control him and stop him from what he was doing, but he slaughtered all of them. Save one. His sister, Tounala, mine and your father's mother.

"Because of this incident, Fae allowed humanity to believe they were evil and were forced to go into hiding. Imprisoned within the Sanctum. They were called demon and devils and cursed. The only Fae left in the open were Valen and his followers. They called themselves the Order and fed on whatever energy they could without replacing it. The energy became like a drug to them. They didn't just need it to survive; they craved it, yearned for it with a deep, intense longing. They wanted it all and, it didn't matter where they got it from.

"They began to prey on humans. They infiltrated corporations, politics, and the government. Creating war, death, and destruction. Eventually, they began killing each other off, leaving only Valen behind."

* * *

Vera waited a few minutes for it all to sink in before she continued. It was a lot for Ryleigh to absorb. She now thought she understood why, when she hugged Cy, he reacted the way he did. There were so many questions, but she wasn't really sure where to begin.

"What happened to Valen?" Ryleigh asked.

"He's dead," Vera replied. Vera stood wiping her hands down her pants to straighten out invisible wrinkles. That was all she offered to Ryleigh for an explanation. "We'll start your training tomorrow," Vera remarked on the way out, and that was the end of the conversation.

* * *

That evening, Ryleigh dreamt for the first time since moving in with Vera.

She was in a dank cave and following someone that she couldn't see. "Hello?" she called out, her voice echoing in front of her, bouncing off of the walls that illuminated her path. It was unlike anything she'd ever seen. Carved into the rock were swirls and symbols unfamiliar to her. From the grooves an iridescent green glow provided enough light to prevent her from stumbling along. A slight breeze caressed her skin and ran through her long dark hair. She felt comfortable here.

The cave felt familiar and safe. Ryleigh felt the air shift and a weight on her shoulder. She turned her head slowly. She wasn't scared. Sitting on her shoulder was a strange creature. It had the ears of a bat with a small squirrel face. Its skin was mottled with purples and pinks.

"Just keep going," it told her.

She wasn't sure what it was, but she knew that it belonged to her and wouldn't steer her wrong. Ryleigh continued through the cave which spilled into a larger room. The cave wasn't a cave. It was, instead, a corridor that led into a room.

"Where am I going?" she asked the creature.

"You know where you are going, Mistress," the creature replied.

"What is your name?"

"You haven't given me one yet," the creature said with a strained sadness.

Ryleigh thought about this, "I will give you a name; it just will take a while to think about."

"Yes, Mistress," the creature responded.

"What-what are you?"

"I am your imp, Mistress."

My imp, she thought. *How strange.* Even though she thought it was strange, Ryleigh knew the imp was there as a companion to help protect her. She thought she could hear sweet music emanating from this imp. Its energy pulsed and matched hers. She tugged at it with her own Chi and could immediately feel energy flow into her. She then realized this imp was more than just a companion; it was a channel, a conduit.

Ryleigh released the flow of energy and looked around the room she was standing in.

It looked as if it were a place for ceremonies. An altar made of stone stood center of the room covered with a dark cloth. Symbols were carved into the rock and she noticed they were the same symbols she'd seen at her aunt's house and on the vehicles that come to visit. The walls were painted dark ochre, and sconces graced the walls with lit torches. To her left she saw a slight movement and continued trying to find whoever it was that brought her to this place.

The place seemed familiar almost as if she'd been here before. She approached the altar and reached out to touch the cloth. She hesitated, fearing the repercussions if she did. She pulled her hand back as if she'd touched an oven burner left on mistakenly.

"It's okay," the imp advised. The moment her fingers graced the cloth, she felt an electric pulse travel from her fingertips and up her arm.

"Is this supposed to happen?" Ryleigh whispered to the imp, knowing it was.

"Yes," it answered. "Yes, my Mistress, it will always happen this way."

Ryleigh placed both hands on the altar, feeling the pulse beat in time with the drumming of her heart. The altar began to glow, increasing in brightness as the pulse sped its tempo. Her heartbeat matched the increased tempo of the altar and her body began to sway with the rhythm she felt. The brightness continued to increase forcing her eyes closed. Ryleigh could feel heat emanate from the brightness of the altar. It crawled over her body. Her skin began to burn more intensely. Ryleigh tried to pull her hands from the altar but was unable to. She tried to yell for help, but she couldn't open her mouth. She tried to open her eyes, but they seemed glued shut. She shouted in her mind for the imp to help her, but it was as if her brain burst into flame and resonated with pain. Her heart sped up with such ferocity it felt as if it were going to explode from her chest. As soon as she thought she couldn't take anymore, a quiet stillness overtook her. She opened her eyes. She couldn't see anything but darkness. She opened her mouth to speak, and all she could manage was a long and loud scream.

11

Discovering who you really are

The next morning, Tristan and Ryleigh skipped school prior to home room. "So, what did she say?" Tristan asked curiously.

He wanted to know exactly how much information Vera was willing to offer up. And if he would be the one, or *should* be the one to fill in the blanks.

Tristan drove them to the same place they were the day prior.

"Vera knows I left school yesterday, she probably knows that I'm not at school right now," Ryleigh said.

Tristan picked up some gravel from the side of the road and threw it into the open desert. "I know she keeps tabs on you," Tristan said. "I'm really not surprised to be honest. It's like she is keeping you as her own private prisoner." Ryleigh sighed as she stood beside Tristan.

"You know that I feel like I know you," Ryleigh started. Tristan stumbled for a moment and turned to look at her. "Just that, I feel like we have a connection. I felt it the first time I saw you in the office." She faced Tristan. "Do I know you?"

Tristan wiped the dust off his hands and wondered if he should tell her the truth. If he did, it might ruin things.

"Aunt Vera also said not to trust you or Illeana, Ryleigh added.

Tristan made a choking sound in his throat, "She did what?"

"She said that you and Illeana would get me into trouble. Do you know what she means by that?"

Ryleigh wanted to know. She needed to know what her aunt meant. If she continued to trust Tristan and Illeana, and didn't at least take heed to what her aunt said, she could be led in all sorts of directions. She didn't know what was right or wrong. She still wanted to know what happened to her parents. What *REALLY* happened to her parents?

"You want to know everything." Tristan hesitated waiting for a response.

Ryleigh nodded. "Yes, I do." Inside a storm was brewing. She was nervous but unafraid. Ready to face whatever Fae would come her way. Or, who might come her way.

"Well, if you want more of the truth, then we need to go someplace else," Tristan headed back to his car. Ryleigh knew she was going to catch hell for missing school. But this seemed more important.

After driving for an hour, they finally arrived at a humble home in a suburban neighborhood. Tristan turned off the car. "Come on."

Ryleigh got out of the car and followed Tristan into the house.

"This is a safe house," Tristan instructed. "My parents bought it years ago, just in case."

"In case what?"

"That's why we're here."

She followed Tristan into the living room. Illeana was sitting on a chair waiting for them.

Illeana smiled, "I'm glad you came."

Ryleigh's storm subsided…somewhat.

Illeana motioned for Ryleigh to sit down. As Illeana spoke, Ryleigh could hear the music in her words. Her voice carried throughout room like the tinkling of piano keys. "Well, first of all, no one can know about this place. It is our family's safe house. It's been warded, protected so that no one can be found inside of it. And since the FPs moved in, we've been coming here, staying here, and have searched through every square foot of this house trying to find any clue possible. We do want to know what Vera told you, and if she told you the truth."

Ryleigh told them about the conversation she had with Vera. She looked at their faces for any signs of truth or deception but they were stoic. They didn't let any hint of emotion out while she relayed what Vera told her. "So, she told me that I need to learn to control this energy. I think I have always felt it."

Illeana nodded, "Yes, you should have. If not controlled, we become enraged easily."

A light bulb moment flashed for Ryleigh, "That is why my dad must have started me running. And why I continue to do it. I feel so much better…as if…as if I can face my day."

Illeana nodded again. "Yes, when we were younger, our parents would make us run and play for hours; but as we have grown, they taught us how to ebb and control the energy we use. But there is something you must know… You have to learn your true form."

"Uh, true form?" Ryleigh asked.

"Yes. What you see before you in the mirror, day after day… that is not who we are."

Ryleigh couldn't help but think about how many times she'd thought her face was not her face in the mirror. How many times did she reach toward the mirror thinking that she was looking at someone that was not her? Someone that was just a mere reflection. She wondered, "If this is *not* my true form, then why in the world do I look like this?"

Illeana laughed out loud, "Because, we're Halflings. We are part human. Our true form, our Fae form, comes with our energy. Once you learn how to use it, then it will emerge."

That made more sense to Ryleigh. "So, as I learn to use my own energy, I'll look how? Like a Faerie? With wings and glitter?"

Tristan and Illeana both laughed, looking at Ryleigh. "No, no, no, no… Not at all. That is why you are here. Tristan and I…" Illeana looked at Tristan, "…we are going to show you ours."

Illeana stood up, and Tristan stood beside her. "We are twins, you know," Illeana began. Ryleigh shook her head, "No, I didn't know that. I was supposed to be a twin, though." Tristan and Illeana looked at each other as if they were communicating silently. Illeana had a habit of scrunching her nose and eyes when she had something important to ask, "You *were* a twin?"

"Yes, I was. I am…I guess."

"O-kay, we'll talk about that in a minute. But for now," Illeana grabbed Tristan's hand, "we are going to show you what our forms are."

Ryleigh sat back in the comfortable blue recliner and waited intently. She thought to herself about how oddly comforting this was. She'd always felt different. She'd always felt as if there were a reason why she never connected with anyone on a personal level. Anyone except Cyrus, and she really missed him.

Illeana and Tristan closed their eyes. Ryleigh could feel the energy in the room heighten as the hairs on her skin started to rise. Illeana's white-blonde hair started to blow as if there were an invisible wind cascading through the room. Tristan's hair didn't move an inch because of the amount of product he used keeping his yellow spikes at attention. Ryleigh secretly thought he was conceited about his looks but would never tell him that to his face.

Ryleigh felt a pulse against her skin. Like a small distinct heartbeat that continued to grow stronger. The flames started to rise from Tristan and Illeana carving their lazy runic patters into their skin. His energy was the violet hue she'd seen before, and Illeana's a cornflower blue. Twins. The same and yet, different.

Both of their eyes were closed and in a breath, their lids opened simultaneously. As they opened their eyes, the flames erupted around them, encasing them in a protective bubble. Tristan's skin became a more translucent and tinged with the violet color of his flames. His eyes were almost fluorescent. He smiled at Ryleigh and she saw rows of sharp teeth. Illeana was similar looking, except her eyes were a stark blue. They were liquid pools of the clearest water. Her hair was the absence of dark as was Tristan's. The absence of all color. Ryleigh was hypnotized by the scene before her. It was cruelly beautiful.

Illeana motioned for Ryleigh to come to them, holding out her hand. Ryleigh wasn't sure if she should. She hadn't yet learned to control the force that lived inside of her, but curiosity propelled her forward. She stepped closer, the pulsing energy between Tristan and Illeana guiding her. Grabbing Illeana's hand, she felt almost a surge of energy shoot through her electrifying her veins. She grabbed Tristan's hand and could feel the connection complete – like a closing circuit. She tried to take a breath but it felt as if she were drowning inside an electrical current.

Inside her mind she could hear Illeana's voice soothing and coherent. *Don't fight it, just allow it to happen.* Ryleigh willed her body to relax. She started to think about when she was running, how her body started to fight when she hit the wall and then adapted as she pushed. She willed her body to push through the uncomfortableness of the situation.

Ryleigh closed her eyes to listen her heart beat and will it to slow down. It became easier to breathe as her heart rate slowed. Counting to herself -- *In-2-3-4, Out-2-3-4* -- was how she made it through the painful moments of running, when her legs wanted to quit and her body fought against her every step. Just four more breaths is all it would take, is what she told her body, willing it to obey her mind. Mind over matter is what her father always said when he was pushing her. Just one more step, just one more block, just one more mile to go.

Ryleigh started to feel a change. Her breathing felt more fluid and she hesitated to open her eyes. *Allow me to show you,* Illeana interrupted her thoughts. Inside her mind's eye she could see herself through the vision of Illeana because of the connection that they were making. A soft illuminescent light cascaded gently over her skin. She could see her skin was a greyish mottled tone and seemed transparent beneath the glow of energy that was surrounding her. Her hair lifted by the energy surrounding the trio was a blood red color. Her eyes were not as translucent as Illeana and Tristan's were. Instead, they were black as pitch. Ryleigh started to panic and pushed Illeana out of her mind. She opened her mouth to speak, and a foreign noise erupted from her throat. It was as if she swallowed a million grains of sand.

Hers, Tristan's, and Illeana's hands intertwined. Now she could see through her own eyes. Through her own Fae vision, she truly saw Illeana and Tristan. She had a feeling that she could see them even if they were not revealing their true form. Ryleigh closed her eyes and thought, *Shut it off,* and could feel the ebb of energy slow down. She felt her insides vibrate as she attempted to pull the energy back inside herself. She wasn't sure if that was what she was supposed to do, but it felt as if were the *natural* thing to do.

When she opened her eyes, she saw Tristan and Illeana staring at her. "How did you learn to do that?" Tristan asked curiously.

"Do what?" Ryleigh was confused.

"Suck your energy back into yourself without a companion." Tristan's tone sounded accusatory. "Are you messing with us?"

"No? No, I'm not. I don't know how I did what I did, but I thought it was what I was supposed to do. What do you mean by 'companion'?"

"You're not supposed to draw it back into yourself, Ryleigh, you expend it through your imp," Illeana commented.

"My imp? What is the heck is an imp," asked Ryleigh. As she uttered the word, two creatures appeared in the room. One next to Tristan, the other beside Illeana.

"These are imps," introduced Tristan.

The batwing-eared creatures stirred. They were just like the imp in her dream. With glowing red eyes, faces like a squirrel, and batwing ears. Their arms and legs were lanky and attached to a small body. They only stood about two-feet high, but it seemed that with each breath they took, they continued to increase in size. Each one's skin color complimented the twins. One was a violet hue, the other the color of the Caribbean.

"You know, "Illeana sounded concerned, "you should have one, too. It's how we dissipate our energy."

Ryleigh shrugged, "I have no idea how or when I am supposed to have one of those."

"You get one once you turn seventeen," Tristan offered. "We got ours on our birthday. But then again, considering how *not* forthcoming your aunt was, you may want to ask her about it."

Ryleigh nodded her head. "Yeah, but what do I say 'Yo, hey, auntie, where's my imp?'" Ryleigh giggled at the thought of walking in the room and talking with a New York accent asking for her imp.

"Actually…that might be what you need to do," said Tristan. "It's not like she has been honest with you. And it seems that she offered up information only *after* we talked."

Ryleigh agreed with Tristan. "Curious. What happens if you take the energy back?" She was wanted to know. It seemed that Illeana and Tristan couldn't do it. So why could she?

"You just – you aren't supposed to be able to do it. You create a free flow of energy that your imp cycles. That's why we were connecting with you, to help you cycle your energy and find your form," Tristan explained. Ryleigh got it. She knew now why he insisted on touching her when creating an energy cycle. He was trying to help her.

"Right, I get that…but, what happens if you do it?"

"What happens when *you* do it?"

Ryleigh thought about that for a moment before answering. She wondered if she should even tell him. Could she even find the words she needed to explain to him what happens when she pulls the energy back into herself? And if she wasn't supposed to do it, why is it that she can? What makes her so special? She never was anything much before, so, why now?

"Well, this was the first time that I did it. So, I don't really know how to describe it."

"Just do the best you can," reassured Tristan.

Ryleigh looked at the twins and hesitated. For a moment she could feel the residual energy pulsing inside her and wondered if it was the same for them. She decided she would wait to find out. She could hear theirs. She noticed the slight difference in tones. She never noticed it before. She imagined it had to do something with what just transpired.

"I could feel you," she pointed to Illeana. "Then I could feel you," Tristan nodded. "Then I felt a connection between the two of you with me as like, a plug?" Tristan and Illeana both nodded at the same time. "Then I could feel my form start to come through. I saw myself through your eyes." She gestured toward Illeana once again.

"And then, once I opened my eyes, I could feel all of us. The pulsing sensation across my skin was electric. Then, I started to feel it get stronger and I needed to… disconnect somehow. So, I pulled it back. And, as I pulled it back… it just… went away."

"Hmm," Illeana walked into the living room and flopped on the couch. Even that was graceful.

"What do you feel?" Ryleigh desperately wanted to know what she was supposed to feel. "I mean, what do you feel when you are done?"

Tristan started, "During, it feels the same as you described. After, I can hear the hum, but that's it. I don't feel it anymore."

Ryleigh nodded, "Yes. It's the same right now." She was lying but she didn't know what she should say. "So, when does my imp arrive?"

Tristan laughed, "You need to talk to your aunt for that one."

Ryleigh knew that was the answer she would be given for now. She wasn't looking forward to having that conversation, but she knew that it needed to happen. This was all the energy work they were going to do for the day but Ryleigh had one other nagging question to ask. "What is the purpose of this energy manipulation?"

Tristan was solemn. "We feed off of the environment, people, places, things… It's who we are, and if we don't, then we are sick. But…we also use it to defend ourselves and also…to heal."

12

Too late to apologize

Ryleigh dreaded having to have another conversation with Vera. She knew she would get an earful for hanging out with the twins when she was told not to.

"I told you to *stay...away...*from Tristan and Illeana," Vera reprimanded.

"Yes, I know, but—"

"But nothing," Vera interrupted. "You continue to disobey me. Were you always this disobedient?"

Ryleigh shook her head. She knew that she shouldn't seem ungrateful. She had an aunt that took her in during her time of need. She should be eternally grateful. "I'm so sorry." Ryleigh was genuinely apologetic.

Vera sighed, "What did they tell you?"

Ryleigh looked at her aunt. "They showed me how to find my true form."

Vera inhaled sharply, "Well then, I guess it's time for your imp. Come with me."

Ryleigh followed Vera into her study and she picked up the phone using the intercom. "Bring them in here."

Siegfried entered the room pushing a steel cage. Ryleigh could hear a soft tittering behind the cloth that covered the cage.

"What's that?" Ryleigh asked.

Siegfried lifted the cloth and revealed a cage of imps. Ryleigh's heart immediately melted when she saw the creatures. There must have been five or six of the small creatures in the cage.

"Why are there so *many*?"

"You have to reach out and see which one connects with your energy, and unfortunately, it is not a pleasant process," Vera instructed.

"Tristan and Illeana didn't tell me anything other than when I turned seventeen I was supposed to get an imp to help me channel my energy."

Vera nodded and agreed, "Yes, this is true. However, in order to find *your* imp, you have to channel energy through one. If the imp is yours, it will live. If not, it will die."

Ryleigh's eyes opened in shock. "I have to what?" she half yelled.

"This is the way it is done. If you have seen your form, then you are ready for an imp. Without one, you can do nothing with your energy. You can do nothing that you need to do to survive as you grow." As Vera spoke, her imp, Jewel, popped into the room.

Ryleigh knew this was something she had to do. She could feel it in her bones. "Okay. I'll do it."

Vera started to explain to her what she needed to do to connect with her imp. Ryleigh would have to cycle her energy and then use it to reach out and touch each of the imps in the cage. Vera explained that she would know when the connection had been made.

Ryleigh closed her eyes and tried to remember what she felt when she'd connected with Tristan and Illeana. She imagined invisible air flow passing over her skin and concentrated on feeling the energy ebb from inside rise to surface through her skin.

She felt the rise of energy like heat, pulsing through her skin and she opened her eyes. A faint glow from the energy permeated the surface of her body, gently gliding over it in waves.

"Now, the imps," Vera instructed.

Ryleigh walked toward the cage where the imps were. She could almost hear what sounded like a small buzzing from inside each of their tiny little bodies. She could hear her own energy harmonious inside her, cascading waves over her body and around her like a shower. She closed her eyes and opened herself to hear the imp's energy as Vera explained. She could tell there were six of them, and as she listened for all of them simultaneously, she tried to tune into the one who matched her own energy rhythm. Vera had explained how to test each imp, she was supposed to reach to each imp and see if they could match the own beat of her Chi. As she concentrated harder, she could hear the pulsating energy from a few of the imps beating at different intervals so she dismissed them entirely and narrowed her focus. This left two imps. She didn't want to kill any of the imps in the cage by trying to cycle energy through one that didn't match her.

She resolved her focus even more. Ever so subtly she began to hone in on a rhythm that matched her own. She could feel its glow, however faint. She took a breath, and as she exhaled she allowed a small stream of energy to flow to the imp. As she did so, she said a silent prayer that it would not harm the imp if this was not the one to connect with her.

As her energy thread reached the imp, it pulled on it and the connection was solidified – immediately. Ryleigh felt a rush of power flow through her and opened her eyes to gaze into the eyes of her imp.

Vera looked at Ryleigh curiously. "Is this the first imp that you touched?"

"Yes," she lied, "I guess I was lucky."

Ryleigh closed her eyes to break the energy connection, however, just when she was thinking to back it off, the flow of energy stopped. This wasn't like when she took back her energy into herself. She could see her imp breathing heavy, and it looked as if it were growing ever so slightly with each breath that it took.

"Don't worry," Vera said "Your imp is okay. This is what they do. They convert the energy and store it for later. They tend to grow a little bigger when they are chewing on it." Vera nodded at Siegfried. Siegfried opened the cage and the imp hopped out of the cage and walked over to Ryleigh's side. "Now you must name it."

Ryleigh thought about this for a minute. She looked down at the imp and noticed that its skin was mottled grey and black. Much like her own when she saw her true form. Its eyes were small and beady with flecks of yellow. The batwing ears were veiny and almost transparent. "I'm not sure what to call it," Ryleigh commented.

"You must name it. It's part of receiving your imp," Vera said.

Ryleigh took a minute and then asked, "Are you a girl or a boy?"

The imp replied, "I am female, Mistress."

Ryleigh smiled. "Then your name is Nissa."

"Yes, my Mistress," Nissa replied.

13

Betrayal

The next morning, Ryleigh didn't run like she normally did; she didn't feel the need to push herself in the normal capacity she usually would. She felt it curious, but remembered the conversation she had with the twins about energy consumption and dissipation. She had used a lot of it over the past few days, and the storm that was usually waiting to break inside her was now a placid lake.

Today, Vera was going to start training Ryleigh now that she had her imp. "I am disappointed that you haven't been taught anything," Vera commented as they walked to another part of the house that Ryleigh hadn't ventured into before.

"I am going to push you as far as I can today. You have to learn to concentrate and listen and hear your body. Each of us has the ability to channel that inside of us. We are able to project it outward in order to protect us." Ryleigh looked at her aunt with uncertainty. They'd entered into a dojo-styled room lined with matts and assorted weapons. Some of the weapons looked medieval with spikes and chains.

Vera saw her niece's eyes widen when they entered the room and laughed, "Don't worry, you will not be learning hand-to-hand combat."

Ryleigh was relieved; she'd never been an intentionally violent person and couldn't even think about swinging a weapon toward another human being. When her aunt advised her the previous night that she was going to start learning how to manipulate her own energy and defend herself, she was prepared to start learning.

"Why *do* I have to learn how to do this?" Ryleigh asked.

"Because," her Aunt started, "there may be those that could harm you." Vera knew all too well the repercussions of others finding out about her. "Trust me, we aren't safe. Not all the time. And now that you have been found, trouble may find us and we need to be prepared."

Over the next few hours, Vera had Ryleigh cycle energy repetitiously through her imp, Nissa. Vera explained that it was important for Ryleigh to make an instantaneous connection with her imp. Ryleigh got the hang of it rather quickly and Vera was impressed. It normally took Halflings their entire lives to learn what Ryleigh was learning in a matter of hours.

By the end of the practice, Ryleigh learned how to pull energy and create an aura shield surrounding her before Vera had the chance to throw what Vera called an energy bomb. The bomb bounced off of Ryleigh's shield and exploded into the wall behind Vera.

"Very, *very* good," Vera explained clearly impressed. "I think that is enough practice for now. I would suggest that you go to the kitchen and have Siegfried make you something healthy to eat and take a nap."

Ryleigh was ready for food and a nap. At the mere thought of eating, her stomach tightened in a painful protest of its emptiness.

Ryleigh was also beginning to also think that Tristan had to have been wrong. Maybe his parents were acting weird because of what was going on? Maybe they were scared? She was meeting Tristan and Illeana later, citing library study as the excuse. She would be lying to her aunt but it was necessary.

* * *

Vera made a mental note to call Fin and fill him in on Ryleigh's progress. He would be pleased to know that she was everything that they hoped for. Ryleigh was beyond important to Finar. Vera wasn't yet sure how much information she was going to relay. Over the phone she could force a non-truth, but in person, that was a feat she wasn't sure she could manage. Vera had always been compelled to answer Finar truthfully and honestly.

If she'd had a witch, that would make all the difference. Unfortunately, they no longer existed. This supernatural natural world they lived in was hard enough without having the right resources. She dialed the all too familiar number, "We need to talk. Face to face." She hated having these discussions with Finar. He could be scary and violent. Her stomach wretched violently. How Adrianne ever dealt with him, she would never know.

* * *

It wasn't an hour before Finar walked into her study carrying an air of arrogance about him. "Well?" he questioned, his dark eyes glittering. Vera remembered how kind those brown eyes used to be.

"She knows," said Vera. She waited for Fin's reaction. He was a slow boil but when he roiled he damn near exploded.

Finar allowed Vera's words to marinate his thoughts. Thinking they could keep her in the dark forever was futile, and he knew she would find out…eventually. He paced back and forth dramatically. It was more for effect than anything. Finar knew it was only a matter of time before Ryleigh realized she was different, or, before someone else told her.

"I am not surprised," commented Fin in his haughty tone. "She is seventeen after all."

"It was Tristan and Illeana."

"Oh really," Fin sneered. I am going to have to have a talk with their *parents*. Trouble. That is what they are." Walking closer with each word until the last was blown onto Vera's cheek with a whisper, "I…don't… need… *trouble*." Spinning on his heel, he tossed his head back. 'I have a contingency plan in action, however."

Vera was afraid of Fin's "contingency" plans. The last time he had a plan, he damn near killed Ryleigh. She told him the car accident was a bad idea, but Fin usually only listened to himself.

"I did tell her I thought her father was alive." Vera regretted the words leaving her lips as soon as they tumbled out. She wished she could have caught them and shoved them back down her throat.

Fin erupted. His true form was one of the most frightening that Vera had ever seen. It seemed as if it took only one step to grab Vera by the arms and pull her close. His eyes glowed red and his skin was riddled with hues of green and blue scales. But his teeth, saber-tooth fangs that hung from his mouth like extended bone. The dark energy that resonated from within him smothered the room in a blanket of filth.

Vera felt as if she were suffocating. She couldn't shift into form. Fin was too strong for that. He pulled energy from her, keeping her form at bay.

Vera started shrinking into the floor whispering, "Stop! Please!" The words choked out slowly with hope he would acquiesce and back down.

He pulled his energy back enough for Vera to pick herself up from the floor. She staggered and fell into her desk, dizzy from the amount of Chi that Fin exerted. The sheer force of Finar's complete form was enough to dampen the output of ten lesser Fae's energy. His form was more demonic. Dark. Ominous. Dangerous.

"If Tristan and Illeana will not stop meddling, then I will make sure they do. Ryleigh. Is. Mine." Finar turned and walked out of the room completely pulling his energy back inside him.

As soon as he left, Vera sat behind her desk with her head in her hands, "What have I done?"

14

The death of a twin

Tristan and Illeana had just arrived home from running errands prior to meeting Ryleigh that evening. They decided they would cook dinner and wanted to pick up a couple things. Before opening the front door, they could feel the air cackle with static. Something was more off than usual. Illeana reached out to turn the handle to the door and Tristan grabbed her hand.

"No," he said. "Let me." Always the diligent "older" brother. Illeana smiled with her violet eyes. They had an unspoken communication.

Tristan turned the handle and the door flew inward out of his hand. He braced his arms to protect Illeana from what danger could lurk inside.

"Come in, children," he heard from the darkness.

Tristan took a step forward, ever hesitantly keeping Illeana behind him. Although they were stronger together, they still needed to be wary of danger.

"Who's there?" called Tristan.

"Don't you recognize your favorite uncle?" the snide voice replied. "Come in here, now."

Tristan and Illeana approached the living room. The smell of sulfur and sandalwood lingered throughout the house, a residual effect from Fading, or traveling from the Sanctum.

Fin was sitting in one of the recliners. He was dressed in his normal debonair style – a relic from the 30s. Finar chose not to update with the modern fashions, instead he preferred pin-striped suits, walking canes, and top hats. His eyes narrowed as the twins entered the room.

"I've heard that you can't stay away from Vera's ward." Tristan moved to speak but Fin silenced him before he could utter the first sound, "Don't. I don't want to hear your excuses. You were warned. You've been warned after the first time you made contact with her. You. Are. Not. To. Talk. To. Her." Fin emphasized each word with a point of his finger between Tristan and Illeana. "I'm afraid I am going to have to inflict some punishment."

"No!" protested Tristan. "She's family! How can we not--"

Tristan's sentence was broken by a gloved hand clasped around his throat. Fin's acrid breath was hot on his face, and Tristan could see the Fae within Fin behind his eyes. Tristan became scared for the first time.

Finar grabbed Illeana by her mane of blonde hair, "I warned you both." They all vanished into thin air leaving behind a slight wind that barely blew dust from the table.

* * *

They reappeared in the Sanctum. The Sanctum was part of the Fae realm. It was what Fae called home after leaving the sight of humanity; a network of caverns filled with memories of the past and echoes of ancestral energy.

Finar still grasped Tristan by his neck and Illeana by her hair. Tristan and Illeana hadn't faded before and were still recovering from the ill effects of it. Fading was harsh on the body the first time, insides felt as if they were twisting into each other as lungs failed to breathe. It was beyond pain.

The twins couldn't breathe and continued to gasp for air. The air was heavier and reeked of sandalwood and sulfur. It could take a few seconds to get used to and was a combination that only Fae could tolerate.

Tristan's eyes burned as he tried to regain his senses and reach for Illeana. He could hear her continuing to cough and gag.

"Ah, ah, ah," Fin remarked. "You two don't get to touch."

Fin propelled Illeana forward into a cell carved from the cave wall behind them. He then threw Tristan into a matching cell a few yards away. Using his energy, he locked the cell doors at the same time. "They are made of ash," he said. "You cannot use *your* energy alone to open these doors. There is iron reinforced through the doors as well. You are staying here until I can figure out what to do with the pair of you." With that Finar disappeared with a pop of air.

Tristan coughed and yelled, "Illeana! Are you okay?"

While very muffled, he heard her respond, "Yes, I'm fine."

He could then hear sobbing. Tristan turned and punched the wall of his cell. *What am I going to do now?*

* * *

Illeana could hear Tristan cursing on the other side of the wall. It sounded distant, but she could feel how frustrated and angry he was that this had happened. She wasn't sure why she was crying. The tears just continued to come and wash her face clean of the settled dust from the cavern. She was angrier with herself...*and* Tristan. They'd just had this conversation. The "What if?" scenarios. This was not what they were prepared for. They had completely underestimated Finar and his abilities.

"Tristan," she called out. "Tristan!"

"Yeah," she heard his voice stifling the anger and disappointment.

"What are we going to do?"

"I am not quite sure yet, but we'll figure out something."

Illeana tried to draw on her inner Chi but she couldn't. There was something dampening her energy. She couldn't even call on her imp to help her out. She tried to stretch her mind out to feel around and see if there was anything, any hope, but she couldn't even reach Tristan to connect with him.

Illeana rested her head on her knees. Her mind tried to run through every possible scenario. She was afraid. Afraid that she and Tristan were going to die.

* * *

Finar was ticked off. It took him a long while to calm down to think about what to do. The twins were lucky he didn't snap their heads off. He did not want Ryleigh to learn anything about who she was or what she could do. He needed her to remain ignorant.

He'd faded into an upper level that contained a home office. It was where he spent most of his time lately. He wanted what lay inside of her, and he couldn't stand to think that she *might* be powerful enough to evade him. He'd already risked so much to come this far. He was one of the most powerful Fae that currently existed outside of the Inner Realm. The hidden realm that no human would ever see where his kind had been banished for centuries.

The Sanctum. That one word was supposed to mean safety…sanctuary…but instead, became a prison. Families living in fear, their kind made to disappear. It was turned into a prison by those who feared the Fae. By those who feared what they could do.

Finar was angry. It was going to be his turn to get back at those that caused their sequester. Ryleigh was the key to it. She held the power that he needed.

"Mia, get in here," Finar snapped.

"Yes, Master," Mia replied as the imp appeared before him.

"Take me to him."

The imp grabbed Finar's hand and they faded out of the upper Sanctum.

* * *

Finar appeared in a cell that was far below where Tristan and Illeana were being held. Each time he appeared before the man, the man grew more and more curious as to why he was not dead yet.

"So, Thomas, tell me about your daughter. What makes her so...*special?*" Finar approached Tom's beaten and bruised body leaning down to whisper in his ear emphasizing the word "special". He was going to get it out of him.

Tom lay on the ground and shut his eyes. Finar looked toward Mia, "Bring her."

It only took a few seconds before Mia appeared with Tom's wife, Adrianne. "You will tell me," Finar sneered as he threw Adrianne on the ground at his feet. She was barely alive. Tom sat up to grab his wife, but Finar kicked him in the chest. Tom muttered a painful grunt as he leaned over trying to recover from pain.

"You don't get to touch her. You may never touch her again...if you don't tell me about your daughter."

Tom rolled over glaring at Finar. He knew that if he told him about Ryleigh, his daughter would be in more danger than she was

S. E. Myers

now. "The only thing special about her," he said between breaths, "…is that she is our daughter."

Finar growled as he grabbed Adrianne by her hair, yanking her from the cell floor. She cried out in pain, grimacing from the torture that had been inflicted on her.

"Please, there's nothing," she implored. Finar threw her behind him and she hit the wall, rendering her unconscious.

"No!" Tom shouted as he lunged for Finar.

Finar grabbed his throat as he came close; invoking his Chi, his eyes glittered as red as rubies as his form started to emerge from his human guise. "I don't think so, Tom. You saw what I did to your companions; imagine what I would do to you."

Tom swallowed hard, remembering the agony he felt as Finar tore his imp limb from limb. The connection to their imps severed, they couldn't channel any energy unless Tom and Adrianne were close and touching.

Tom looked to his wife, limp and unconscious. Guilt flooded through his being. He knew he needed to give Finar something, anything…he just didn't want to be forced to divulge the truth. He couldn't put his daughter in that kind of danger, but no matter what he told Finar, she would be a gross target. He could only hope that, once he exposed her, she would have learned enough on her own to ward off the danger heading her way.

Finar moved toward his wife. "You have exactly three seconds. I know you moved away to keep her hidden. Keep her secret. And you are going to tell me why if you want yourself and your wife to live."

Tom winced, knowing he had to speak up or he and his wife would die. He didn't trust Finar, but he knew he could buy him and his wife some time. "Okay. I'll tell you what is special about her."

Finar looked pleased; his Chi pulling back inward, his imp breathing hard from being unable to control the amount of energy Finar had the capability of exploding. "Get on with it then."

"We believe that Ryleigh absorbed her twin's energy. That's why we moved away. That is why we ran."

Finar immediately looked interested, and a small slow grin crept along his face. He knew what that meant. It meant that Ryleigh was even more powerful than even she could imagine. Two in one. Those infants were usually slaughtered at birth. There were tests to be done. But first, Finar needed to speak with Tristan and Illeana. They were the ones who were teaching Ryleigh what she was.

Finar turned to leave, ordering Mia to return Adrianne to her cell.

"Wait!" Tom requested. "Let us go!"

Finar laughed. "Did you really think I would let you leave? Let you leave now?" Mia appeared back in Tom's cell. "We'll see what we can do *after* I test your daughter. " With those words Mia hopped onto Finar's shoulder and they faded back to the upper level of the Sanctum.

* * *

Tristan was in his cell trying to figure out how he could possibly get Illeana and himself out of this situation. He wasn't quite sure, but he thought he noticed Finar's imp, Mia, display the ability to fade in and out of the lined cells. He thought about Ryleigh and his insides screwed up. He felt screwed up for even having feelings for someone he just met and that he was supposed to be related to. But there was a connection, and he was pretty sure she felt it, too. But this wasn't anything he could think about now. How related were they anyway? He shook away those thoughts. Family is family.

Tristan paced the length of the cell and examined the structure. The walls were smooth and rounded. As if a bubble created the space. He placed his hand on the wall to see if he could pull any type of energy reading from his environment. He felt nothing but rock. His hand glided over the rock, feeling the smoothness and coolness of the face. He was worried but didn't want to show it. It was only a matter of time before Finar came back and punished them. He just wasn't sure what type of punishment he was going to inflict.

The space was illuminated by artificial energy at the crest of the ceiling. The ceiling had to be at least twelve-feet tall. Tristan knew he couldn't reach the top, but he attempted to jump anyway. Even with practicing *parkour*, he could not reach that type of height without a vantage point. *Damn him!* He couldn't even call on his imp to help him out. He tried sending an energy thread to attempt and touch Illeana. Nothing. The ash and iron were dampening his ability to use his Chi. He couldn't even reach inside himself to make an aura shield. For the first time, he felt naked and vulnerable.

As if on cue, he could feel the energy in his cell collapse. Finar faded into view, and Tristan backed up into the wall. He wanted as much room between him and Finar as possible.

"So, how do you like your accommodations?" Finar asked with a laugh in his tone. Finar emphasized each question melodically, "Comfy? Cozy? Does it remind you of home?"

"Oh sure," Tristan dripped with sarcasm. "Just like mom's home cooking." Tristan narrowed his eyes as he stared down Finar. "What do you want from us?"

Finar glared at Tristan. "You think you're cute, don't you?"

Tristan shrugged, "Maybe. Maybe not." He almost dared Finar to hurt him. He wanted him to hurt him.

"You don't want to tempt me, young one. I am not one to be tempted," Finar cackled and snapped his fingers. His imp appeared with a folding chair.

Finar flipped his coat tail and took a seat. "This is how it is going to work." Finar twirled his cane in his left hand as he glanced down and then over to Tristan meeting his eyes. "You are going to tell me *everything*, and I mean everything you taught our dear Ryleigh."

"And if I don't?"

"Then I will kill your sister," Finar said matter-of-factly. And he would. He would kill Illeana in a split second. Tristan knew it.

"What do you want to know?" Tristan asked. He would only give him enough information to save their lives.

"I want to know everything. You choose to tell me what you feel everything is. I will know whether or not it is."

Tristan glowered at Finar. "Where do you want me to start? I don't know what it is you want!"

Finar was up and across the room so quickly, it looked as if he disappeared and reappeared in Tristan's face, "You start with what you and Illeana were teaching Ryleigh. That...is what I want to know, youngling!"

Finar punched the wall next to Tristan and shattered the rock. Pieces of the chipped rock flew into Tristan's face leaving small cuts and droplets of blood. Tristan reached up to touch his face and looked at Finar who was back in his chair. The wall crushed under the pressure of Finar's fist leaving a hole that molded his hand. Tristan looked across the room and he was sitting in the chair twirling the cane as if nothing happened.

As much as he didn't want to, Tristan had to release some information. "We just helped Ryleigh find her true form," he said meekly.

"And? What is her true form?"

Tristan didn't know how to explain what happened in the house. "She's... different. I...I don't know how to describe it."

"Well, maybe your sister knows how," Finar challenged. "Shall we ask?"

Tristan shook his head. "No." Taking a deep breath, he exposed Ryleigh for what she was without realizing it. "Her energy is different. She doesn't need an imp to channel."

"What does she look like?" Finar needed to know. There was only one way to know.

"Her eyes, they are black as pitch. But her energy...her energy is as pure as the dawn."

Finar stood from his chair and snapped his fingers. "Mia. Vera."

And with that, he faded away.

Tristan turned and punched the all where Finar's fist had been. He pummeled the wall until his knuckles were bloody and raw, knowing that what he did may have saved him and Illeana. But he also might have condemned Ryleigh. Condemned her to die.

15

Was it really love?

Vera wasn't aware that Tristan and Illeana were taken by Finar already. She was still trying to recover from the dampening of his energy in her room. Using sage, she smudged the room in its entirety. When this venture started, she wasn't sure what was going to happen. She knew that she felt a connection to this child that was her ward. She'd tried to stay disconnected from her. But the truth was, she did love her. This was her niece, the only connection that she really had to her brother.

She didn't even know where her brother was, but she knew he was alive. She could still feel the connection to him inside her.

Finar scared her. He didn't used to. He used to be kind and loving. When he started researching his lineage, he realized that there was a way to become more whole instead of the Halfling he was. He never liked the idea that they were who they were because of the human race. Discovering that he was a descendant of Valen and that Valen was his father made all the difference.

Fae truly disassociated themselves from any human contact. Although their children attended normal schools, once they reached maturity, they no longer had communication or were "friends" with any human. That interaction was strictly forbidden.

Vera remembered when Finar was actually interested in her. He was supposed to be her mate. Her brother with Finar's sister, Adrianne. And she with him. Anytime he was around, the attraction to him was intense. It was almost beyond her control. She felt cheated, robbed that she was unable to share a life with her mate. Her mate that is now determined to become more than what he is now.

Ryleigh was his salvation, he said multiple times. He knew that there was something special about her. She assumed that this was why Tom and Adrianne left. Why they disappeared. There was something that they never said or told anyone. Vera didn't even know that Ryleigh existed. She never knew that her sister-in-law was pregnant. She didn't even know that Ryleigh was a singular birth. Fae are always born in pairs. There is a twin and the two make one.

It was as if the dots connected. Vera should have realized. She should have known. She knew that Finar wanted Ryleigh and that he wanted to taste the Chi inside her. She realized that he wanted what Ryleigh had. Ryleigh had double the amount of Chi, making her more than a Halfling. Making her whole Fae. She had to see for herself before Finar came back. She wasn't sure how much time she had left before Finar returned from whatever it was he was doing.

Ryleigh was still sleeping upstairs. "Siegfried!" Vera called panicking, "Get the car. We need to get Ryleigh, and we need to get out of here now!"

Siegfried walked into the room with a grimace on his face.

"Humans," a familiar, taunting voice called out from behind Siegfried. "I never understood why you employed them."

Siegfried fell to the floor face first. Finar stood behind him with Siegfried's heart in his hands. Dropping the heart on the floor, he gracefully stepped over the body. The heart made a sickening wet sound as it landed on the wooden floor. "Now, dear, where *are* you going?"

Vera's hand covered her chest as if to keep her heart from bursting out of it, "I, uh..." She swallowed, "I needed to run some errands."

She tried to keep her face smooth and free from the distress she was feeling. Finar stood there for a moment with his head cocked to his side. His dark glittering eyes looking her over. She could feel his gaze penetrate her.

"Really?" he replied sarcastically. "Is that all you were doing?"

Finar loved to draw out his words for effect. Each word was like a cliffhanger. Vera could smell the sulfur and sandalwood emanating from his body. She knew that he had been through to the Sanctum. It was where he spent most of his time, and she could only imagine what he did there. Vera didn't like it. She didn't want to be where memories from the past haunted her kind around every corner. Reminders on the walls in paint and blood. She would rather forget and move on. She survived this long, she was sure she could survive this moment with Finar.

"Yes." she stood up and straightened her outfit. Today was a casual day. Jeans and a nice blouse with top of the line heels. As casual for her as it would get.

"My dear, you know what would happen if you lied to me?" Finar approached Vera and caressed her face.

Vera longed for his touch. She allowed her eyes to close for just a moment so she could feel his energy connect with hers. Her eyes flew opened suddenly when she realized her mistake.

Finar jerked back as if disgusted by the touch of her. The disgust on his face was apparent. "Ah, you little minx. You know you can't lie to me."

He always used her to his advantage. Knowing that if he touched her she would open to him. It was like truth serum. All he had to do was touch her and she would melt in his embrace. Even in his cruelest moments she still craved his touch.

Before Vera had a chance to back pedal out of the situation, Finar changed forms. His Fae side erupted in a smoldering heat.

Vera closed her eyes just waiting for the moment to pass. She didn't want to feel the enduring pain but knew that she would.

"I'm so sorry," she whispered.

Finar came close, kissing Vera ever so softly on the cheek leaving blisters where his lips touched.

"Oh, my Vera," his now gravelly voice echoed in her mind, "how I loved thee." He placed his palm on the center of her chest and started to draw out her energy. Vera's body flung back limp, the life force trickling into Finar's palm.

Vera's skin turned ashen and wrinkled as her Chi ebbed into Finar. Finar's skin radiated from the intake of Vera's energy. He threw his head back and a roar erupted from his belly. Absorbing the energy was painful as it intertwined and attempted to match its rhythm with his own. He dropped her body as he clutched his chest with his claw-like hands. He fell to his knees, embracing the back of his neck.

Vera was not as weak as she made herself out to be, and as her energy melded to his, he started to feel the residual effects of her memories. The memory absorption splintered through his skull leaving him sightless for a few moments. However much more powerful this made him, it still was an intolerable pain. As this form subsided, his nose started to bleed and drip onto the floor. He looked over at Vera's body feeling a second of remorse for this woman who was supposed to have been his mate, but he would find another. He was sure of it, once he absorbed enough energy, he could have anyone he wanted. And anything. He sniffed and wiped his nose with the back of his hand as he rose slowly. Feeling the meld happen satisfactorily, he stepped over her body and Siegfried's and left. Before Ryleigh, he needed Tristan.

"Mia," Finar said, exhausted. Mia hopped onto Finar's shoulder and they faded back to the Sanctum.

* * *

Tristan was sleeping soundly when Finar awoke him with a swift kick to the ribs. He couldn't even focus before he realized he was being dragged out of his cell. He tried grabbing the arm that was pulling him forward, but he was having a hard time moving. Tristan realized that he was tied down with rope, so he attempted to use his Chi to burn through and loosen them.

"That isn't going to work," said Finar as he continued to drag him. "You've been bound to the ropes."

Tristan attempted to ask him what was going on, however, he was unable to speak.

"Ah, yes, can't speak either. Makes it much more bearable for me if I can't hear you scream," Finar said matter-of-factly. "Luckily for me, I have a witch at my disposal."

Tristan tried turning his head around to see what was going on. He could hear a female voice mumbling something he couldn't quite make it out. Finar continued to drag him out of his cell and into another room. Finar flung him into a chair in the center of the room. Tristan glanced around as much as his eyes would allow, he noticed Illeana facing toward him on his right. He looked at her pleadingly with his eyes to see if he could pick up a glimmer from her at all, however, he could read nothing. Nothing at all.

Finar stepped into his view holding something in his hands. It looked as if it were a silver goblet with some type of symbols engraved around the chalice. He heard the female voice behind him say, "Drink."

Tristan looked at Finar who now held the goblet in front of his face. "Drink." Tristan shook his head. Finar's eyes turned into their ruby clusters. "Drink it now." Staring into Finar's eyes he knew he could not refuse. Finar placed the liquid to Tristan's lips and he took a gulp. The strange liquid burned the inside of his mouth, his throat, and continued into the pit of his stomach. He choked trying to gulp air while trying to swallow the mixture down.

The burn traveled from his belly through to his arms and his limbs, becoming a warm numbness. His head started to feel lighter and airy. Inside he felt as if everything were right. If it was the way it was supposed to be.

He didn't feel wrong.

Finar glanced at the red-headed witch behind Tristan. "Is he ready?"

"Yes," she replied. "He will do as you wish."

"Good."

Finar dragged Illeana's chair toward Tristan so they were facing each other. "Tristan," he grabbed his face forcing focus on him. "Tristan. You are going to do what I say, right?" Tristan nodded as Finar talked to him.

"I need you to connect to your sister," Finar said, placing his hands on her shoulder.

Tristan was fuzzy. He felt as if he were supposed to do something else besides listen to this man giving him instructions. He closed his eyes and reached out to connect Illeana. The drink that Finar gave Tristan, infused with calamus and mace, was combined with a spell to make him more pliable and bend to Finar's will. The drink also gave Finar the ability to magnify Tristan's power by touch. As Tristan tried to connect with Illeana, Finar grasped him by the shoulders to enhance Tristan's magic.

Finar wanted to see if he could combine Tristan and Illeana's energy. Tristan reached out to connect with Illeana, his energy synched and harmonized with hers. As they were connecting, Finar reached through Tristan, enhancing the strength of his Chi and increasing the frequency in which it was speaking to Illeana.

Illeana was spelled and open to any magic and all energy requests around her. Anyone at this time would be able to connect with her. She was vulnerable. Her guard was down. All because of the witch's magic spells and potions.

Finar knew what he was doing. He knew that once Tristan absorbed his sister's energy, she would die. He was curious to see how Tristan would react. Would he completely absorb her energy, enhancing his own? Would he become whole Fae? Or would he remain a Halfling with twice his power?

Finar encouraged Tristan's energy stream to pull on Illeana's gently. Tristan became more unaware of his surroundings or what was happening. The only normalcy he felt was the ebb and flow of energy between him and Illeana. He had more energy flowing toward him than she had flowing back toward her, but he didn't realize it. Everything around him was passing by in what felt like slow-motion, however, it was only a matter of seconds before Finar increased the energy exchange and started pulling mass consumption from Illeana.

Illeana threw her head back, writhing in agony as her Chi was being ripped from her body. Finar watched the transition greedily as brother was feeding from sister. He was enthralled, feeling the energy transference beneath his hands. Illeana's eyes flew opened and her mouth hung slack jawed. Finar recognized the signs.

Her skin started to fade to a greyish tinge and her cheeks became hollow and recessed. Her body dropped and continued to become limper with each Chi pulse outward. Finar could hear her heart rate begin to slow and the hum of energy dissipate.

The last pulse of energy flowed from Illeana through to Tristan. Finar released his grip and waited for what would happen next. He expected to witness the painful sensation he experienced each time he stole and absorbed the Chi of another Halfling.

He waited for it. Tristan just sat there, still numbed by the liquid and magic that was given to him that he ingested.

Finar turned to the witch grumbling, "You said this would work!"

"Give it time, it will work," the witch reassured in her honey-smooth voice.

Moments continued to pass as slowly as molasses in the dead of winter. Suddenly, Tristan opened his eyes. Groggy and distant, his violet eyes clouded over as if he were staring into a distant horizon. In one split second, his body began to seize and almost fold itself backwards. His arms and legs stiffened as his jaw tensed and flexed. His eyes were still open. Rolling onto the floor face first, his body rigid, groaning noises erupted from within that continued to grow louder.

The room's energy started to grow thick, and Finar threw an aura shield surrounding himself as a just-in-case. The witch behind him started muttering an incantation for a protection spell. Finar had a suspicion that, no matter how much magic she used, it would not shield her from what was coming. He wanted to see exactly what would happen, so he stepped out from in front of the witch. His eyes glittered with excitement.

Spittle erupted from the sides of Tristan's mouth. And then blood. Finar started to get a little nervous. He could see the rivulets of blood running from the corners of his mouth, down his cheek, following gravity to the cell floor. Finar wanted to reach out and touch him, but he knew better than that. He knew that he couldn't or he might get pulled into the mesh, the intertwining, and it would end badly. With as much energy as Fin had already absorbed, he could never be what he thought Ryleigh was, or what Tristan was possibly becoming.

The seizing continued for a few seconds more until the blood was just a small trickle. The energy died down, and the room started to cool. But then…the inner hum of Tristan's became louder with each progressing heartbeat. Finar started to back away from Tristan until he was against the wall in the cell. He could feel it louder and louder and rising in pitch continuing to increase in intensity like the percussion section of an overture. The witch's eyes turned into glass saucers. She hadn't been prepared for this.

"Let me out!" the witch screamed at Finar as she started toward him, pleading.

Finar lifted his palm towards her and halted her in her tracks. She started to scream frantically, feeling the energy begin to shift in the small room. Tristan's inner energy began to manifest outwardly. Violet hues with tinges of Caribbean, a blend of the twins Chi curled and rose with each heartbeat.

Tristan's body rose from the floor as the flames continued to gather underneath him. This was what Finar was waiting for. His personal experience was always excruciating, but this was what he truly yearned for.

Tristan's body seemed to writhe with the flames and his skin danced beneath the flames. A translucent hue, shaded by violets and blues, created the darker purple that painted his skin like mini rainbows. The groaning ceased. Tristan was silent, but his body seemed to be wracked with pain.

The concoction Finar gave him was also created to mute the pain he would feel. He could see it didn't work – completely. For a youngling that never experienced this type of pain, he was a lot stronger than Finar gave him credit for, and he'd certainly expected long, loud, and arduous screams. As a matter of fact, Finar was slightly disappointed that it didn't happen that way.

The flames spilled from Tristan's body and onto the floor pooling around him. His body rose sitting him in an upright position. The flames began to cascade from his body and onto the floor. Continuing to move around the cell, they consumed everything in their path, including Illeana's body, leaving ash behind. Finar began to wonder if his aura shield would be enough when Mia appeared, strengthening his protective barrier.

The witch, however, was in the direct path of the flames. Her blood-curdling screams were an indication as to how potent Tristan's Chi had become. Her body melted into the heat, feeding the energy and making it stronger.

When they blaze reached Finar, the pinnacles of heat were tremendously strong. In the shadows, Finar could see Tristan's form change. No longer were his eyes a violet hue, they were an absence of light. His razor-sharp teeth were emphasized by the hardened skin, glimmering against the light of his aura. His hair was still clear and standing on spike like ends.

The flames lapped at Finar's aura shield. Mia channeled the energy from outside of the Sanctum to add power to his shield in order to protect her Master. If the flames penetrated the barrier, Finar would be dead.

He could feel the strain on Mia. "Master?" Mia sounded fatigued. "I cannot hold it any longer."

Finar's disappointed washed his face in the growing light. He would be unable to witness the full transition. He knew that Tristan would be able to leave the Sanctum on his own and wanted to count on that. He had slowly devised a new plan of action, and it was coming together nicely.

"Get us out of here," he commanded, and with that, the pair faded out of the Sanctum as the entire cell erupted into a violent beauty, leaving Tristan to complete the transformation on his own.

16

It's a new day, It's a new you

As his consciousness started to push through, a migraine shredded his senses. Tristan rolled over and grabbed his head, crying out in agony feeling the throbbing pain of the headache pulsate behind his eyes. All he could do was scream and hold his head, containing its contents, preventing it from exploding.

The agony lasted for what seemed an eternity, but in reality, it passed within moments. As soon as he was able to recover, he pulled himself to his knees. His memory was fuzzy after Finar came into his cell. He did remember being dragged on the floor and forced to drink something, but after that, the memory faded out. He looked around the room for clues, the smell of ash and soot was heavy in the air. Bits of the floor were still smoldering. Then he noticed his clothing.

He was standing completely naked. His clothes were gone. Only remnants of the material were glued to his skin with the soot that was left behind.

He noticed piles of ashes throughout the cell and the cell door burnt away, exposing the slightly melted steel rods. Waves of nausea rocked through his system, and he fell back to his knees, vomiting the contents of the drink that Finar gave him. Wiping his mouth with the back of his hand, he noticed the blood.

He felt off. Different. He didn't know why. With the door open to the cell, he needed to see if he could summon Vee and get back home. He also needed to find Illeana. *Where was she?*

Tristan was having a hard time focusing. He made it through the door and sent a thought to his imp before collapsing. Vee appeared at his side and then took him back to his safe house.

* * *

After Ryleigh woke at home, she immediately made her way downstairs and snuck out of the house. She was supposed to meet Tristan and Illeana that evening and decided not to bother checking for Siegfried or Vera. She wanted to avoid all questions regarding her whereabouts if possible.

Hours had passed, and Ryleigh was still waiting in the safe house. She'd flipped through the channels on T.V. for about the millionth time and contemplated going back home. Each time the house made a sound, she jumped. She wasn't scared, she was nervous. It was unlike the twins to leave her hanging, and besides, this had been their idea. She'd tried calling both of their cells, but they didn't answer.

She decided to talk to her imp Nissa. They hadn't really bonded yet, and Ryleigh thought that she should get to know her. Ryleigh wanted to know about her abilities, what the imp could do, and what Ryleigh was supposed to do.

"So," Ryleigh started, "what exactly are you?"

"I am an imp, Mistress," Nissa responded, her large eyes sparkling with curiosity.

"Yeah, I know that," Ryleigh said. "I guess I wondered more like where do you come from?"

Nissa jumped on the couch next to Ryleigh and sat down. Her arms, legs, and head were larger than her torso. She almost looked like a puppet without strings. "I am born just like you," the imp explained.

"Do you know who your mom and dad are?"

"No, Mistress. I am just born, and then I was picked."

Frowning, Ryleigh questioned, "How long were you – were you in that cage?"

"I don't know," Nissa said. "I was just one place, then another. Then you picked me and now we are together." Nissa's voice was soft and melodious.

Ryleigh nodded. She'd been thinking about the training session she'd had with Nissa and how the energy fluctuated between them. Ryleigh likened it to turning on a faucet, slowly. It trickled little by little until there was a steady flow.

While Ryleigh was lost in thought, Vee appeared with Tristan smoldering in the middle of the living room floor. Ryleigh smelled sandalwood and sulfur, and Tristan's nakedness was showing through the soot.

"Nissa, "she ordered. "Get a blanket!" Ryleigh knelt next to Tristan on the floor. "Is he alive?" she asked Vee.

"Yes, he is alive. Just barely," Vee said mournfully. His small voice normally higher pitched was low and slightly inaudible. "Something is different."

"What do you mean different?" Nissa appeared with a blanket, and Ryleigh covered Tristan.

She had Vee help her pull Tristan onto the couch, and then she fetched a bowl of water and a washcloth to clean off his skin.

"He feels different to me, Mistress. I also could not find Illeana or Gori." Gori was Illeana's imp.

Ryleigh wanted to know what Vee meant by Tristan "feeling" different. She tried reaching out to Tristan with a thread to connect to him, but as soon as she attempted to do so, she was rebuffed. It felt as if there was an invisible wall that prevented her from reaching inside of him. She listened to his thrum of energy and heard a different tune than what she'd heard before. It wasn't the same tempo. It didn't sing to her like before. He sounded familiar, but there was an underlying tone that she couldn't identify. She continued to wash him off, tending to his wounds and finally allowed him to rest.

* * *

Tristan's dreams were disturbing. Finar was standing in front of him commanding him to kill his sister, but he refused. At least in the dream he did. Tristan dreamt he sucked the life out of her, that he pulled all of her energy into him.

Illeana appeared in his dream "Oh, my dear brother," she said, sadness dripped from each word spoken.

"Where are you?" he cried. "I can't find you. I can't feel you."

She was ethereal beauty. While her face was angelic, she was ferocity at its finest. Her beauty shown through like a lighthouse in a summer storm.

She touched his face with her graceful fingers. "I am with you. Always." She wiped a tear escaping from his eyes, rolling down his cheek. He closed his eyes reveling in the touch of his twin. He knew she was speaking the truth. He knew that she would be with him always.

"Shhh now, brother. You have so much you are going to need to do. Ryleigh needs you. I need you." She turned away from him. He could feel the tether that connected the twins drifting apart.

"Wait!" he cried. "Don't leave me; I can't do this without you!"

She looked back at him, tears streaming from her eyes, "We are one now." She placed both hands on his head and forced back the memories he couldn't remember, undoing the spell the witch laid upon him.

Tristan woke up screaming.

* * *

Tristan rolled off the couch clutching the sheet that was covering him. Tristan didn't know where he was until he saw Ryleigh rushing in the room.

"Are you okay?" she asked breathlessly.

Tristan wasn't sure if he was okay. His heart was pounding through his chest and it felt as if his head were going to split wide open. "I… I don't' know." He sat down.

Ryleigh reached out to touch him, but he pulled away. "Vee says… Vee says you're different."

Tristan nodded.

"What in the world is going on?" Ryleigh wanted to know what happened to her cousin. To her friend. This was the only person she had grown to trust and she needed to help him.

Tristan held his head steady in his hands. Ryleigh waited for him. She could feel his sadness permeating the room. The vibrational energy shifted, and she could hear his internal hum slow down. The strange underlying tone was what she wanted to know about. Why was he different?

He took a big gulp of air and hesitated before saying, "Illeana is dead." The pain stabbed through each word as it rolled from his tongue.

Ryleigh was shell-shocked. Her heart ached for the relative she'd known for only a short time. She loved her. She couldn't possibly imagine what Tristan was going through. The loss of his sister, his twin that he was with since birth. They had never been separated. Hot tears streamed down her face and Tristan turned to look at her.

"I'm so sorry," Ryleigh said. She reached out again, and this time he didn't flinch away. She held him tightly as wracking sobs shook his entire body and her with it.

"You…you don't know what I did," he cried in-between breaths.

"Shhh, it's okay. You didn't do anything."

"No!" Tristan screamed. He pushed Ryleigh away abruptly and stood. He started pacing the living room. "I did it! He made me. He made me take her into me."

Ryleigh was bewildered, "Who? Who made you do what?"

Spitting the name from his mouth with such hatred and venom it was almost as if he was cursing, "Finar."

"Finar?"

"He gave me something. He had a witch. I…I don't know…it is still all fuzzy."

"What do you mean that he had a 'witch'?"

"In the old days, witches and Fae worked together. Magic and Chi flowed together. Where there were Fae, there were witches. When Halflings started to make their appearance, they started practicing witchcraft in order to increase their power. They wanted to match their Fae counterparts, however, when the Elders found out about this, they stripped all Halflings of their ability to work magic.

"There were natural witches about, those born of the craft. The Halfling Fae began to seek them out until the Elders banned that also. Imps were the ones who were usually called in order to find witches. Imps aided witches with their craft. Because imps belonged with and were paired with Fae, they were the ones who sought them out. All witches were eventually killed and imps became paired with Halflings to assist them with controlling their Chi.

"Finar had a witch that did something to me. Illeana told me. I mean, I dreamed that she told me. I – I don't know. "Tristan was confused and angry this was happening to him. He wasn't quite sure what was going on and he wasn't in his right mind. Ryleigh brought him some food, "Thanks. I need to wrap my head around this."

Ryleigh nodded and allowed him to eat in peace. She decided she would jump on the computer to see what she could find out about Fae/witch interactions. It seemed that all the research Ryleigh could find related to combined witches and faery and imps were tied to folklore. Imps and Fae helped witches with their power – for favors of course. If a witch needed a spell, or needed an herb, there were always Fae to help. Those favors usually resulted in children. True witches could not have children, not on their own. Not truly on their own.

17

Connecting

Tristan finished eating, changed into sweats and a t-shirt, and sat on the couch staring into space in disbelief. After his dream, a thought crossed his mind. "Ryleigh," he called her into the living room. "Can you help me with something?"

"Ah, sure… what do you want to do?" she asked him, unable to mask her confusion. He'd just gone through hell; she thought he would want a little more time to recuperate.

"When Finar made me…" Tristan trailed off. It was hard to admit, that he killed his sister. "When he made me take Illeana into me, I think he was trying to make me…whole."

"Whole?"

"Yeah, as opposed to a Halfling. I need to connect with someone. I need to see what's different. If anything at all."

Ryleigh was more than willing to help and Nissa was getting used to the amount of energy Ryleigh could pull through her. Tristan knew that if things got out of hand, Ryleigh could break the connection and pull away from him.

Tristan sat in the middle of the living room floor. Ryleigh sat across from Tristan – facing him.

Tristan put his palms up facing Ryleigh. "Illeana and I used to do this to practice cycling energy without our imps. Sometimes the draw could really drain them, and we would rather that we were exhausted instead of them."

Ryleigh took a deep breath and placed her palms against his. They both closed their eyes.

"Concentrate on my breathing," Tristan instructed. "As I breathe in, you breathe out and vice-versa."

Ryleigh could hear his breaths, slow...intentional. As he let his air out, she took it in. Cycling breaths helped with cycling Chi. It was a way to regulate the ebb of energy they would send and receive.

As the breath beats continued, the energy humming beneath Ryleigh's skin began to tremble. She felt Tristan and heard the tune of his Chi rumbling in his core. Opening their eyes, they attempted to send energy from one to the other as they were breathing. As Ryleigh breathed out, she sent a tendril to connect with Tristan and he did the same. This cycled the energy between the two, carrying

Chi from Ryleigh to Tristan and back again. The temperature in the room began to rise. Vee and Nissa paced back and forth feeling a rumble beneath their rabbit-like feet.

Tristan and Ryleigh were locked in an eternal dance that continued to spiral and syphon each other's Chi. Ryleigh could feel the difference in Tristan, the strength in his own core and thought she could even feel the presence of Illeana. She knew what he meant now by the two becoming whole. Tristan recognized Ryleigh's presence. He also felt that she was more than herself, but she didn't have two vibrations, she only had one where his had the melodic undertones of Illeana.

He pushed a little harder, allowing a little more of his own Chi to cycle into Ryleigh. Ryleigh did the same. This was the same practice for younglings. It helped them practice control and also understand how much energy an imp could take when they received one. Tristan wanted to see exactly how much energy he had and how much he could cycle.

He pushed again, harder this time. Ryleigh felt the intensity of it and accepted what he was flowing into her. Ryleigh mirrored his actions, but she also sent little bits of Tristan's own energy that was melded with hers. On the exhale, he attempted to do the same, but found he couldn't. He couldn't expel her energy.

Tristan absorbed whatever she gave him and started to pull faster. It became uncomfortable for Ryleigh as a ripping sensation generated from her solar plexus. With their energies conjoined, it became more and more difficult for Tristan to sever the connection.

Tristan started to panic because he couldn't control the flow of energy.

His eyes pleaded with Ryleigh, begging her to shut it down. While connected, speaking was improbable, and their psychic link was distorted because of Tristan's anomaly.

Ryleigh got the message and concentrated on the energy he was pulling from her. She figured that, if she blasted him with enough, it might break the connection. She imagined a ball of light at her core increasing in size. As the ball grew brighter in her mind's eye, it grew brighter in front of her and started to stunt the flow of her energy to him and cycled only his back to him.

She continued to concentrate on the ball of light, attempting to solidify the mass. *Don't be mad!* She thought as she pushed the mass toward Tristan.

The impact shot Tristan backwards into the couch and was enough to break the connection instantaneously.

Nissa immediately jumped into Ryleigh's lap, providing her a replenishing supply of energy. Ryleigh was breathless and gasping for air.

Tristan sat forward grabbing his chest. His face was riddled with pain while he focused on recovering from the energy blast. "I knew...you could do it...I needed you to do it."

Ryleigh was still gasping for breath. "What – was – that?"

"I'm not sure, but...I think I am like you...and not."

Ryleigh shook her head and wondered what he was talking about. "What do you mean like me?"

"You are more, more than just part Fae. I think that is why Finar wants you."

"Finar wants me? Why would he want me?"

"I'm not sure," Tristan replied. He lied to her. He had a feeling that Finar wanted to do to Ryleigh what he made Tristan do to his own sister.

"I need to talk to Aunt Vera," Ryleigh resolved.

She needed to make a trip back to the house. By now, Vera would be pretty ticked off that she wasn't home. Her cell hadn't gone off, which was a bit concerning – she figured that, by now, Vera would be hounding her every thirty seconds.

Ryleigh absentmindedly stroked Nissa's ears as Nissa was healing her. Nissa didn't mind at all. She actually liked it but didn't want to say anything. Although she was a lower caste Fae, she was still more powerful than these younglings. Nissa had the ability to heal, to hurt, and to cause destruction. She was growing to love her Mistress. She loved the attention she got. She knew some of the other imps didn't get the same attention she received and was saddened by it. But they had no choice once they were bonded with their Masters or Mistresses. So, for now, she reveled in it.

18

What is the truth?

Once recovered, Ryleigh knew going back to the house was probably a mistake. Tristan and Ryleigh decided to go together. They were going to use the imps to fade into the house and back.

The plan was to get in and get out. Ryleigh knew that Vera and Fin were connected. She *wasn't* sure whose side Siegfried was on, but she was sure it was with Vera.

Tristan wondered about the FPs and his real parents. "I just don't know if my parents are still alive."

He was also slowly coming to grips over killing his sister. It was hard, and it tore him to the core, but knowing that Finar made him do it gave him something else to focus on. Having Illeana's energy within him also provided him comfort. He'd started noticing her voice in his head, telling him it would be okay and he was reminded of the dream. "I'll be with you always," she'd reminded.

They were ready to go. Tristan and Ryleigh figured that if they connected their Chi, as dangerous as that could be, they could stand up against Finar if he approached them. Tristan grabbed a switchblade and handed it to Ryleigh.

"I have *no* idea what I would do with this," she remarked.

"Well, if worse comes to worse, you face the pointy end away from you and make stabbing motions at the one attacking you. It has worked for me in the past, I'm sure it could work for you," Tristan said half-jokingly.

Ryleigh took the blade hesitantly, hoping she wouldn't have to use it.

"Okay, we're ready." Tristan motioned to the imps.

They linked hands, and just like that, they were in the mansion foyer.

Ryleigh handled fading for the first time like a pro. She collapsed to the ground only for a moment before regaining her stability.

The house was almost as she left it, Ryleigh thought. But it felt...off. She turned to Tristan and mouthed, "Something feels wrong."

He mouthed back, "I know. I feel it too."

There was residual grime in the air that coated their senses. Ryleigh grimaced at a horrible smell that curled her upper lip and roiled her stomach. Tristan could smell it too.

The initial plan was to sneak into the study. Ryleigh had a feeling that, because Vera spent most of her time in the study, there might be some sort of clues lying around.

They headed that general direction and Nissa whispered to Ryleigh, "Be careful. I can feel him." By *him*, Nissa meant Finar. She could feel whose energy was used last, and she could really feel the pull of him.

Ryleigh motioned to Tristan, "Nissa says to be careful." Tristan nodded.

Tristan went toward the study door and froze. He saw Siegfried first.

He turned around to Ryleigh. "Siegfried is dead."

Ryleigh pushed Tristan sideways and saw for herself that he was lying in a pool of his own blood. There was a hole in his back that showed floor beneath it. She shook the nausea away. Determined, she pressed into the room.

She moved to step over Siegfried's body, Tristan grabbed her shoulders to pull her back, but she shrugged him off. Then she saw her. Vera. She was nothing but a shell. Her skin was the color of smoke and looked as fragile as rice paper. Ryleigh covered her mouth and made a muffled cry.

Tristan came in behind her. "Ryleigh, I'm sorry." He was genuinely apologetic. Although they believed Vera had an ulterior motive, she was only family that Ryleigh had left, besides him.

Ryleigh knelt beside her body.   Her entire body seemed as if it were just sucked dry. Ryleigh reached out to touch her one last time, and as she did, Vera's body turned to ash.

Ryleigh jumped back, crying out in shock. Tristan grabbed Ryleigh and pulled her into his chest. Ryleigh sobbed for a minute before Tristan refocused her. "We have to get moving. I know Finar did this, and we don't know if he will be back here…for you." Ryleigh sucked in a deep breath and in and decided she could mourn later.

They headed for the desk.

Riley started going through the top drawers, pulling them all the way out. She'd seen too many movies and detective shows that showed a false bottom or area where people never looked. She noticed a book with the same sigil she'd seen everywhere else.

She opened the smooth leather cover. *The Diary of Vera Whitmore* it read. "I found her diary," she mentioned to Tristan. He turned toward her and away from the filing cabinet he was rifling through.

Ryleigh continued to thumb through the journal. "It's just her private thoughts. There is a lot here; I will have to go through it later. Are you finding anything?"

Tristan shook his head, lying. Tristan decided he would come back later…without Ryleigh.

They continued through the drawers, and before walking away from the heavy mahogany desk, Ryleigh decided to run her hand underneath the main drawer. She felt a button and pressed it.

Behind her, a door swung open from the bookcase. Tristan and Ryleigh both were curious to know what was behind the bookcase, but Nissa spoke up, "That's the way down."

"The way down?" Ryleigh asked.

"Yes, Mistress. It's a portal...to the Sanctum"

Tristan had explained to Ryleigh the place where he was but only faded there and back. "Vera didn't have an imp, and this must have been the only way for her to access it," He offered.

"Why not?" Ryleigh asked.

"I am not sure, but we don't want to go there yet. I am sure that Finar has to know someone is here now if the door has been accessed."

"Then I guess we better hurry." Ryleigh clicked the button to close the door.

Back at the safe-house, the two were extremely disappointed. They tried accessing Vera's laptop, but couldn't figure out the password so they brought it with them. Tristan tried to show outwardly how disappointed he was, but he had to get back to that house without Ryleigh.

Ryleigh was exhausted. "I think I am going to rest for a bit," she told Tristan.

He muttered a response as she left, and decided that he would go back now. It was as good of a time as any to retrieve the files he'd found. He knew he would find more information about his parents. It was something he simply had to do.

"I am going to go out for a bit," he called to Ryleigh.

Ryleigh looked at him with dead determination. "You need to stay safe."

He would stay safe alright. That was his intention. To keep him…and Ryleigh safe.

19

To find out for one's self

Tristan felt kind of guilty that he didn't tell Ryleigh where he was going, but he had Vee with him and that made all the difference. Tristan's self-assurance could be his downfall. He never thought about the consequences of his actions. He knew it was a risk, but it was a risk he was willing to take. Obviously something happened that made Finar leave him alone in his cell and risking the chance that he might escape

"Well, Vee, looks like it's you and me this time," he told his faithful companion.

"Yes, Master, it is," the imp said.

He was always willing to help, but it was also his duty to protect his master. Although Tristan had changed inwardly, Vee had the capability to match it. Because Tristan and Vee both matched their energy during the selection process, Tristan originally wasn't sure if he would be able to cycle energy through his imp any longer. However, because his twin's vibrations matched his own and were only slightly different, Vee was able to handle it.

"Let's go to Vera's," he said, and Vee faded them back to the mansion.

Tristan hesitantly stepped back through the door. Fading was becoming easier, it was much like swallowing the medicine you hated to take as a child that your mother promised you wouldn't taste so bad. After the first couple of spoonful's, it starts to taste like normal, and you forget about the ugly shudder you have after the swallow. Ugly shuddering aside, Tristan was feeling much better than he had for the past couple of days.

After enduring the torturous side of Finar, he was ready to meet him. He was hoping he would know he was here and stop him from finding out the truth. He wasn't going to enter the Sanctum; he wanted to go back through the files. While rifling through them earlier, he saw his family name. He wanted…no, he needed to know and understand the truth about what was going on.

He re-entered Vera's office, her ashes on the floor and Siegfried's body left to rot. He motioned toward the mess. "Vee, can you?"

The imp nodded and immediately got rid of Siegfried's corpse and Vera's ashes with a flash. Meanwhile, Tristan turned his attention to the filing cabinet he'd rifled through earlier. He saw the files he wanted to glance through. Simmons. Young. Rayme. Their family names. Ryleigh's parents changed their last name to Simmons when leaving to protect her. And Finar, he never used his last name…Young.

He wasn't sure where to start. He sat at Vera's mahogany desk and laid the files in front of him. He closed his eyes and sat in silence for a moment.

He opened Simmons first. A copy of birth certificates, mortgage documents, loan applications, pictures of Ryleigh when she was an infant through her age now, her parents wedding invitation. It looked like Vera was starting a collection. She hadn't known about them before, had she?

Whitmore. Vera's file. Tristan only found one document, but it was in a foreign language. He was sure it was some type of European language and would take that with him.

His file. Again, copies of birth certificates, mortgage documents, leasing contracts, pictures, phone numbers, and school information. The file was about an inch thick and would take time to go through. Tristan wondered what was so important. Why were *they* so important? It didn't' make too much sense to him at all.

He ruffled his spiky hair and sat back thinking for a moment. Then he heard something behind him. He thought it was the swing of the door. He started to turn, but it was too late. The *faux* parents grabbed him and pushed him to the floor.

"What do you think you're doing?" the faux-mother said.

"Get...off... of me!" Tristan shouted as he struggled to break free of their hold. He didn't want to pull his energy yet. He just wasn't sure what he could and couldn't do.

The faux-father stood over him looking down, "Not yet. Finar wants you and is very upset that you didn't appreciate how gracious he was."

This ticked Tristan off. He closed his eyes and tried to quite the rumble that was growing inside of him. He wasn't even sure how the faux-mother was holding him down, but he was determined to get back up and defend himself.

All Fae were trained from the time they learned to walk on how to physically defend themselves. Tristan was calling upon that recollection of memories.

The faux-mother holding him down was unbelievably strong. Tristan had the advantage. He knew he was much stronger than her. She was pinning his arms down and using the remainder of her weight to sit on his chest with her knees on his shoulders. He just needed one second.

When Tristan opened his eyes, they had changed. They were no longer the pretty purple color that reflected his soul. They were darker, blacker pits that showed the hatred he was feeling. He wanted these FPs to tell him where his parents were.

The faux-mother looked down. "Oh crap!" she said unexpectedly.

The faux-father stood above Tristan and became extremely nervous. This was the moment he needed. He bucked his hips, throwing the mother up and over his head into the father. He rolled in one swift movement to rise to his feet. Standing his ground, he pulled himself as tall as he could. He could see the fear in their eyes.

"Where are my parents?" he demanded.

The mother looked at him strangely. "We are your parents." She swallowed hard.

"Do not piss me off. I don't know what I'm capable of, but I see that you might."

He took a few steps forward for good measure expecting them to cower. And cower they did. He was pretty impressed with himself. He smiled and he saw that fear in these people who were not his parents.

"I know you are *not* who you say you are," Tristan spat with venom. "You need to tell me where they are....now!"

The father stepped forward. "I don't know where they are."

As soon as he said that, the guise fell from their faces. Before Tristan stood new faces that he did not recognize.

"Why are you here?" Tristan asked, the anger building with each passing moment.

"Finar...Finar made us. He has our children."

Tristan wasn't sure whether or not to believe them. The father looked sincere as he said it, and the mother was distraught.

"How many?" Tristan continued to interrogate.

The mother replied, "Two. My twins. My girls." She allowed a small sob to escape between her lips. Tristan's heart lurched, but his gut told him they were lying.

"I just don't believe you. I can feel lies slipping off your skin."

The distraught mother's face screwed up tight, "You don't know what the truth is!" She started for him, but the father grabbed her as she began to shriek.

"Calm yourself, Sam!" he shouted.

Sobbing, she slipped from his grasp and fell to the floor. "I want my babies back." She looked mournful and truthful. Tristan had the upper hand. Did they know he would really incapacitate them?

The father said, "My name is Cael. My wife, and she *is* my wife, is Sam."

Tristan sucked his form back in and returned to normal. "And your children?"

Samahara sucked in a sob. "Katarina and Kaelyna. My girls. They are only seven."

Tristan was a surprised. Twin girls? Halflings were always born as opposite sex and *never* the same sex. He sighed. This was not what he expected. "Why does Finar have them?" He was curious. Why was he targeting younglings and those coming of age?

"Because he wants us to do his will," Cael remarked. "He needs help to accomplish his goal."

"And, what's that?" Tristan was a little surprised with the amount of information he was receiving. It seemed as if it was too good to be true.

"He…he wants you. He wants Ryleigh. He made you more Fae." Cael continued to explain the situation to Tristan. "When Fae are born, they are usually born twins. I know this isn't new to you. Either we are sterile or we have a set of twins. It is how we maintain." Cael started pacing the room, "What Finar found out, is that twins can absorb one another. It is rare for a singular birth. Very rare, but Finar found one a few years ago. A boy who just came into his Faehood. He was the boy of an old family."

Cael paused for a long moment. Just as Tristan was about to speak, Cael continued.

"When he came into his Fae hood, his Becoming, things started to happen. He didn't need his imp to channel any energy; he was able to take everything he dished out back. His parents did what they were supposed to do. Teach from the time the baby was able to walk and start showing signs of using Chi." Tristan nodded. Sam stopped sniffling to listen to the story. It was one that she had heard a few times before. "Finar immediately started to show an interest in him. He started showing up and offered to mentor and tutor the boy. Then we noticed changes in his behavior. Jonathan became withdrawn and even started to lose weight. It wasn't until it was too late that his parents and the Elders found out what Finar was doing. Finar was siphoning energy from the boy; it's not unusual to share energy of other Fae. We do it often; however, he wasn't giving any back. He was almost *feeding* from him."

"This was unheard of, even in the Fae community. " Tristan nodded his understanding. "Then Jonathan disappeared.

Accusations started flying toward Finar's direction. When the council convened to decide what to do, Finar interrupted the meeting. He was – more. He was more Fae. He was more powerful." Cael shuddered when he remembered what happened.

"How do you know all of this?" Tristan wondered. But he was not prepared for the answer that he received.

"Because, I am an Elder. I was on the council." Tristan hadn't met an Elder before. They were to be treated with respect and dignity. Ceremony aside, Tristan needed the answer he craved most.

"Where are my parents?" he asked.

Cael's face turned to one of regret and sadness. Tristan knew the answer; he just didn't want to admit it. "They are dead, Tristan. I am so sorry. I promise, we didn't kill them."

Tristan swallowed, refusing to allow any more emotion to pour from him. He pushed it down into the pit of his stomach, letting it stew with the other rage and hurt that he was saving. He would release it, but not today.

"We are so sorry, Tristan. Truly," Sam echoed. "We had no choice but to pretend to be your parents. Finar threatened us and took our girls."

"The only reason he hasn't yet killed me is because I have information that he needs," Cael said.

Tristan wanted to ask what it was, but before he could speak the words, the doors to the study exploded open. Splintered wood flew everywhere like bullets raining down. He heard Sam. Cael backed up in front of Tristan.

"My, my, my…are we having an *un*family reunion?" Finar asked snidely. He had Mia with him and a few other imps that Tristan was unfamiliar with. "You know," Finar's eyes gleamed with deviousness, "Your parents were brave until the very end, Tristan."

Tristan could feel the anger start to build inside of him. Cael placed a hand on his chest. "Not now, he's doing this on purpose. You have to control yourself."

"Oh, Tristan, don't listen to Cael. You know you want revenge," Finar continued to goad him. "You know," Finar started. "You killed that witch. The one who helped me drug you."

Tristan glared at Finar. He clenched his fists wanting to blast him into oblivion. He could feel his nails digging into his palms. Feeling the pain was ebbing away the anger.

"Where are our children?" Sam demanded. Her true form gleaming through. Her skin was mottled with golden hues and a tail whipped ferociously behind her. Her hair was like glass shining through red wine. Cael stared at his wife and then back to Finar.

"Oh, Sam, your girls are safe. And don't worry, they have so many years ahead of them."

With those last words Sam emitted a sound, high-pitched and deafening to human ears. She created a fireball in her palms that reached the size of a basketball and flung it at Finar.

As the ball reached Finar, he caught it and passed it back and forth between his own hands.

"Did you really think that would work?" he asked Sam. Cael was in his true form in a blink. As soon as he reached out to touch his wife to increase their power, Finar flung an energy web, covering Cael to prevent him from reaching her.

Finar laughed. "It doesn't really matter what you do. I will win. I have consumed too much energy. And, Tristan, once you realize that you can't fight me, you will join me."

"I will never join you." Tristan replied.

"Oh yes you will."

Before Tristan could react, there was an explosion. Vee felt the energy increasing in the room and prior to the pinnacle; he already started creating a shield surrounding Tristan and attempted to fade him out of the study. The explosion demolished the study and collapsed the bookcase guarding the portal into the Sanctum. The concussion from the explosion knocked Vee flat and threw Tristan into the wall. Cael and Sam were demolished in the blast. Their ashes left blowing in the wind.

* * *

While Tristan was away, Ryleigh began to read Vera's diary. She felt bad for deceiving him; however, she wanted to have an opportunity to read the journal without him.

Opening the pages, she took a breath. Even though Vera wasn't the most welcoming, she was her family, and Ryleigh was saddened by her death. Instead of starting at the beginning, Ryleigh skipped to the end. She wanted to know what Vera was writing or thinking since she moved in.

The Diary of Vera Whitmore

October 21st –

I still miss him. I wish that he and I were still together. Unfortunately, due to circumstances and this disconcerting quest that he has taken upon himself, that cannot be. Still, I need him in my life no matter how much it hurts.

He twists me inside like no other could. He is my mate. Supposed to be my mate. I don't understand what he wants with Ryleigh. It just doesn't make sense to me.

October 24th –

Finar just left. He was furious with me. I could feel that his energy has changed. It no longer sings to me in the same tune it did before, and he seems very disconnected. Ryleigh disobeyed me and started hanging out with Tristan and Illeana. I'm afraid they've revealed to her what she truly is.

I was a little surprised to find out that she was not aware of who she was. Her parents sheltered her from birth. I can still feel Thomas. I know that he is not dead. I know that Finar has him and I am sure it is in the Sanctum. A place I cannot go. My imp cannot take me there. My family line was supposed to be the protectors of the Sanctum portal. And now Finar is using it for his own devices. I should have never shown him. The Elders will be furious with me.

Today, Siegfried told me that he suspects that Ryleigh is more than what she appears to be. I don't question Sieg anymore.

He was been with me for years and years. Finar still believes he is a human in my employ, however, if he ever found this and ever found out what Sieg truly was, he would kill me.

I am beginning to truly love this child. I wish she would open up more to me and ask me more questions. I don't know how much I could ever reveal, but I would help her best that I could without Fin finding out.

November 1ˢᵗ –

Dear Ryleigh,

If you are reading this, it is because I am now dead. I don't have much time, but I need to tell you this.

You were supposed to be a twin. I think that you might have absorbed your twin's energy while in the womb. This would make you more a whole Fae born. I don't know if my suspicions are correct, but I believe that is why Finar wants you. You don't need your imp to help you. You are special, my darling. Very special.

I hope you find this in time. You need to learn how to control your power. You can defeat Finar, only you can. He will try to kill you or use you, or both.

You should also know that Tristan and Illeana are not your cousins. You are not related by blood at all. Let them help you as much as they can, I fear that you will need them in the future. Tristan was supposed to be your mate, but Finar didn't want you two connected. He wanted you for himself.

Find your parents. Find them quickly.

Know that I love you, and know that your father is still alive. I can feel it. If your father is alive, there is hope that your mother might be, too. I am truly sorry for everything. I hope that we can get away in time.

Always,

Vera

20

The realization of a romance

The more she researched, the more Ryleigh began to understand why her parents kept all of this information from her. But did they really help? Or did they just retard her ability to make a decision for herself. There was so much she didn't know and so much she still needed to learn.

The internet with its wonderful unending vastness and wealth of information were her crutch. It didn't answer all her questions and sometimes created more that needed to be answered. Lilin – defined to be demonic children of Lilith. Each born with varying abilities, super human, super powerful. According to Vera, these were all lies. Ryleigh didn't want to believe this was what she was.

Waiting for Tristan and tired of being cooped up in the house, she practiced cycling energy through Nissa to gain a faster connection. Nissa was learning to control Ryleigh's ebb and flow of energy. Nissa was becoming a pro at it, and Ryleigh was learning her limits. Any more than that, she was afraid to do without Tristan.

The wards protecting the house prevented her from being located by Fae charms. No matter how hard Finar tried to find her, he would not be able to locate her or her imp.

Ryleigh thought of Illeana and chased the thought away. A sob caught in her throat. She swallowed it down. If she began to dwell on it, she would get angry and she needed to use that. Instead, she thought about everything she needed to tell Tristan. She needed to tell him how she felt. She never felt so sure about anything in her life. Before they walked into Fin's trap. Before the possibility of her death or his happening, she needed to tell him how she felt and what it meant.

As if on cue, Tristan entered the house. He was dirty and bloody and looked as if he had lost the fight to a few of Finar's bullies.

Ryleigh rushed over to him, "Are you okay?" She glanced him over, but he wasn't bleeding anywhere that she could see. She looked at Nissa who looked him over and concurred that it was not his blood.

"Are you okay?"

"I'm fine," he offered a small laugh. "You should see the other guy." Wincing as he stood up, he walked into the kitchen.

Ryleigh decided not to wait. "We need to talk. I've done some research."

Tristan turned to Ryleigh. "You have my full attention."

Ryleigh closed her eyes for a second to clear her mind and think about how she was going to relay all of the information that she just found out. "I just don't know where to start...yet."

"What's the most important?"

"You were right about Vera keeping tabs on me," Tristan said with a nod. "She started to track where my mom and dad moved around to, she even had information about my birth." Ryleigh turned away from Tristan, "Absorbing my twins energy...my Yin to its Yang... makes me more whole than any other Halfling. Two in one."

Tristan staggered back as if he were going to pass out.

Tristan fell to the floor realizing what Finar made him do. Ryleigh followed him to the floor and hugged Tristan tight. She covered him with a warm flow to calm him. She could hear the soft gentle hum of Tristan's energy flow. She so wanted to send a thread to connect with him, but she was afraid of what he might do; so instead, she was content to try to comfort her grieving friend.

She grabbed his face to look into hers. "Tristan, there's something else. He looked at her with bloodshot eyes. She knew the pain he was feeling. "I know this doesn't even matter now, but – well - we are not related."

Tristan cocked his head to the side, "What do you mean?" he asked.

"Well, according to Vera, we are not related. We aren't even from the same family."

"Why would they even tell us we were related if we weren't?" questioned Tristan. He was confused, hurt, and just wanted to sleep.

Ryleigh wasn't sure if she could even speak the words. She mumbled a few words that were difficult for her to even hear.

"What?"

"Because you and I. We were supposed to be together." Ryleigh finished barely above a whisper.

"Wait...what?" Tristan sat up and slid with his back to the cabinets. "We were?" he motioned between the two of them.

Ryleigh nodded.

Tristan sat there for a moment. Ryleigh could feel the energy in the room start to thicken and glanced at Tristan. His eyes were on her. That lovely shade of violet that haunted her dreams. Her body started to respond to the energy Tristan was sending out. The hairs on her pale skin started to rise. Her jet black hair danced with static. Tristan reached for Ryleigh's hands and she gave them to him. Nissa and Vee were on the kitchen cabinets just watching. They knew this ceremony. Even though they were young, the genetic memories were there.

As soon as they touched, Ryleigh closed her eyes listening to the thrum of energy that was around her and recognizing it was Tristan's. She felt Tristan send an energy thread towards her – she did the same.

Ryleigh opened her eyes. She thought for a moment how wrong this was. But that it wasn't.

Tristan and Ryleigh were locked in an eternal gaze. His eyes translucent violet and hers a translucent green. The Chi thread, normally invisible took shape displaying the intertwining, melding of their Chi.

The drumbeat of Tristan's energy sped up to match Ryleigh's and hers slowed down to match his. As their energy melded, the room became electric. The lights flickered and furniture shook. Palm to palm they knelt. Their faces inches from each other looking as if they were attempting to drown in the other's gaze. The imps rocked back and forth from one foot to the other. Nervous and jittery. This was different.

Ryleigh whispered, "Tristan."

They lowered their palms and he grabbed Ryleigh around the waist and pulled her into him. She leaned her head into his shoulder breathing him in as he did the same with her. With each inhale he would exhale. They were one. She lifted her head to gaze into his eyes once more and met his lips instead.

His lips were all she had imagined – soft and inviting. Their kiss seemed to last for an eternity. The toaster exploded behind them, but they did not hear it. Ryleigh reached her arms behind Tristan for an embrace. They continued to cycle energy through each other until Tristan pulled away.

Ryleigh followed suit and pulled her energy back inside of her. Tristan still needed to use Vee because he hadn't learned how to reserve and pull it back inside himself since absorbing Illeana's.

Ryleigh smelled something burning and turned to look around. She noticed the toaster smoking and stood up slowly. All the light bulbs around her exploded. She jumped and screamed as each one popped. Anything that had been plugged in was no longer in working order.

Tristan laughed a little and said, "I knew this moment was going to happen."

Ryleigh looked at Tristan, "What do you mean?"

"The first time we met."

"In the office?"

"Yeah. Do you remember getting shoved?" Tristan asked her.

"Yes," Ryleigh said slowly. "I do."

Tristan laughed, "It was Vee. I think he knew the whole time. Didn't you, Vee?"

Vee looked at his master happily. "Yes, Master, I did know. I did."

Ryleigh smiled at Tristan. "I am glad I don't have to feel as if what I am feeling is taboo anymore. I am a little fuzzy right now though."

"Don't worry, it will pass."

"I think I knew that." Ryleigh smiled.

21

To become a tracker

"Her journal said to find my parents. I need to find them. Vera felt that my father was still alive."

Tristan nodded. "I would imagine that, if your dad is alive, your mom would be, too. Finar more than likely will use them against you."

"I know. I think I'm ready."

She really wasn't sure if she was ready. She was scared. Out-of-her-mind. She was just getting used to this idea and everything was happening too fast. She could feel the end coming, and she felt sick to her stomach. She knew she needed to save her mom and dad. They needed to confront Finar and do something about him. But she just wasn't sure what. She knew that Tristan wanted to kill him for what he'd been compelled to do. She was prepared for that, but she wasn't sure what or how she could handle dealing with it if her parents were dead or she couldn't find them.

"I think I am ready. I really do," she told Tristan. "But…but I am really scared."

Tristan pulled her into a tight embrace, sending warmth over her body. "I am scared, too. I am. I am also pissed. You need to push it down inside. "He pulled her to look in his eyes. "Push it down and save it. Use it when we need to."

Ryleigh closed her eyes and attempted to quell her fear. She breathed deep, pushing it into her core until she felt nothing. She looked at Tristan. "Okay."

"Let's go."

Tristan and Ryleigh packed their backpacks with all of the supplies that they might possibly need. Typical Ryleigh – always prepared. Once done, Vee and Nissa alighted on their shoulders and pulled them into the Sanctum.

* * *

Ryleigh felt as if her insides were being pulled through her belly button. By the time she opened her eyes, they were there. Sandalwood and sulfur invaded her senses and she doubled over to puke.

She wretched until her stomach was empty of its previous contents. She hadn't expected that, and Tristan didn't tell her. It took a few minutes, but Tristan allowed her to regain her senses.

She stood up and drank in the scenery. It wasn't anything that she imagined. When she thought of a prison for her kind, she imagined flames and chains; instead she was greeted by cave walls and gardens of strange plants.

They called them Fae, but they weren't fairy-winged creatures in children's stories. They comprised of beings of all sorts. The purveyors of energy. They kept things grounded and together. They assisted and helped humanity, and then they were thrown into prison because of Valen. And now, Finar was just like his own father. Tristan and Ryleigh had to save her parents and kill Finar. But they weren't even sure where they were going or even if they could.

"I saved you that night," Tristan admitted. He figured it was as good a time as any to come clean.

Ryleigh gave him her raised eyebrow, "What night?" She wasn't sure what he was talking about.

"The night of the accident. Mia came to me and told me about you. I saved you."

Ryleigh stopped walking for a moment and looked at him. "You knew? You knew this whole time?"

"I-I wasn't sure exactly what was going on, "he continued to explain. "Mia said there was a girl who needed my assistance and faded me to the road." Tristan took Ryleigh by the shoulders and looked into her eyes in all sincerity. "By the looks of it, you were almost dead, but I could feel the energy inside still ebbing and flowing without a heartbeat."

"What did you do?" Ryleigh asked.

"With the help of Mia, I was able to save you and bring you back. You had a metal rod shoved through your abdomen, we healed you and brought you back." Tristan turned away, closing his eyes, thinking about the alternative, "Had your energy been gone, you would have been gone. You'd have been in the nether."

"The nether. A place where their energy dissipated. Some believed that once one passed into the nether, they returned another time. Much like reincarnation. But in the nether, they sometimes would not return."

Ryleigh started to remember her dream. The caves, the incantations. She knew that, for whatever reason, this was where she was supposed to be.

"I've been here before," Tristan looked at her strangely. "Well, not physically, but I dreamed of this place before."

"That has to mean something." Tristan started to wonder about Ryleigh's abilities. Premonitions, extra sensory perception…this was not unheard of among the Fae community. Usually, they left those abilities to the witches. They were used to channeling the energy in order to provide help and healing to humanity. They helped build the communities that they lived in, but the witches had the premonitions and ability of precognition. Precog was not predispositioned for the Fae. The Fae were healers and creators. They were the building blocks of life. The energy they siphoned helped create life, prevent death, set balance, and even brought those back from the brink.

"I don't know what it means, I only know that I am supposed to be here, and I've been here before."

Ryleigh started to feel a little bit of pressure in her chest. Maybe it was a little bit of nervousness. Tristan grabbed her hand to reassure her. He could feel how shaken she was because of the connection they now had. Because they were threaded together, they shared more together. This was a connection that they would never be able to break, unless one of them died.

Ryleigh remembered Vera's diary and reading about how much she was connected to and loved Finar. She remembered how much she longed for that. And now…now she had that with Tristan. She'd had it before she even knew what it was. Now she understood why she'd felt so incomplete before. That or it was because she was supposed to be a twin. The void she'd felt before, her entire life before this, was now filled.

Ryleigh was ready for whatever was to come their way. She felt a pull, almost an urgent need to move forward. The detail inside the cavern was incredible. The walls were chiseled, and yet, they looked as if it were man-made instead of stone formation. Six-foot stalactites seemed as if they might crash to the floor at any moment. On the tips of each stalactite, were points of light that illuminated the pathway. Strange and beautiful plants lined the walkway with burnt orange and purple hues. Ryleigh was entranced by the beauty around her.

Tristan also felt a pull, but he was feeling it through Ryleigh. He grabbed her arm. "Do you know where we are going?'

"No," she replied quietly. "But I feel it. Can't you feel it?"

Tristan didn't answer her. Ryleigh sounded as if she were in a trance almost, -- drugged by this place and its undercurrent of tones and music that it played. Tristan couldn't hear or feel it. He could only sense it, and that was only because of his connection with Ryleigh.

He followed her down the winding path. He hadn't seen the rest of the Sanctum when he was released from his cell and didn't know where they were.

They could feel another presence around them, watching them move forward. Ryleigh didn't want to call out and find out who or what was there. She wasn't even sure what the Sanctum held or the types of creatures or Fae that would be present. Nissa was still sitting on her shoulder and grabbed her hair tightly.

Ryleigh knew this was just for reassurance, because Nissa was a little uncomfortable. This was Nissa's home, and if she were worried, maybe Ryleigh should be, too.

Ryleigh stiffened and Tristan stopped. "What is it?" he asked.

"Don't you feel it? Something is coming."

It was something. Something large and dark, lumbering towards them, headed their way. The smell of Sulfur continued to increase in strength. Tristan told Ryleigh, "Get ready."

Nissa and Vee moved behind the pair and grabbed hands to help the cycle of energy they may need to fight. Tristan took his form, and Ryleigh stood there silently watching as the creature continued to move forward.

The creature was a shadow with glowing yellow eyes peering from a place where its head should be. When it opened its invisible mouth to speak, the smell of rotting fish escaped its body. Ryleigh almost tossed her stomach – again.

"What are you doing here?" the creature asked, slurring each word and placing extra emphasis on the vowels. "You are not allowed." The creature stood there, waiting for an answer.

Ryleigh was the brave one. "We are looking for …Finar. And my parents."

The creature laughed aloud, deep startling sound that reverberated throughout the room they were standing in. "You younglings are all the same."

"Can you help us?"

The creature's eyes narrowed to slits and were barely visible as it looked at Ryleigh and Tristan up and down. It noticed Tristan in his form and raised a globular hand to point at him.

"There is no need for that here," it said. "No harm will come to you."

Tristan backed down and waited for an explanation.

The creature hissed each word that came through the stench of its mouth. Loud baritone tremors echoed through their body as he talked with them. He explained that younglings, as they are still called, are never to be harmed as told by the Elders.

The Elders. Ryleigh read about them in the diary. They were the rule makers, the keepers of secrets, and the ones who should be able to help.

Tristan and Ryleigh told the creature why they were there and about Finar.

"Can you take us to the Elders?" Ryleigh implored. "We need help. We need Finar killed, locked away, anything. He is dangerous and killed my aunt."

Soulebad, as the creature was called, thought for a minute before replying, "I can talk to the Elders. I am sure that they can help you. But, you must wait here."

Ryleigh and Tristan agreed to wait and Soulebad sauntered off to speak with the Elders.

As soon as Soulebad rounded a corner, Ryleigh was moving forward.

Tristan hesitated. "I thought we were going to wait."

"I'm not waiting. I'm going to find my parents." With that, Ryleigh followed her gut and went the opposite direction of Soulbad.

* * *

Tristan had no choice but to take Ryleigh's lead. Pushing forward and taking the opposite path of Soulebad, the pair ventured into the darkness sparsely lit by the lights above. Ryleigh was unafraid. She felt...okay. She knew that if anything harmful happened, she would be able to make it and survive. She only wanted to find her parents.

They continued along the path forward and felt other beings – creatures watching them. They dared not show their faces because they knew what she and Tristan were about. This empowered Ryleigh, gave her the courage to press forward and keep going. She was the epitome of strength. She felt as if she could take on the world.

Tristan also felt a little empowered. He could feel the creatures surrounding him, not venturing to find out whom or what was invading this space. This Sanctum.

He continued to trust in Ryleigh and followed her. They seemed to descend multiple levels. The Sanctum was complex, full of twists and turns. They only ventured along the paths, trusting in Ryleigh's instinct.

Tristan stopped. "This is where he kept us."

Ryleigh stopped as well. "This is where he kept you and Illeana?"

Tristan nodded and started to feel anger rise within him. He swallowed hard, feeling Illeana inside him, her energy calming him. Tristan would have his revenge.

Ryleigh stood fast for a minute. She wanted to see if she could reach out and feel her parents. Concentrating on the love she felt for them, she could almost see them in her mind.
She felt them both. "I know they are here," she said confidently. "I can feel them here. Just not...here." She pointed around the cells and sighed. "I don't know where he could have kept them."

Tristan had an idea, but he wasn't quite sure how Ryleigh would react to it. Splitting up was never good in these types of situations; however, it was something that they needed to do in order to cover more ground.

"We should split up," Tristan suggested.

"You're right," Ryleigh responded shocking Tristan. "It's the only way that we will be able to cover the most ground."

"Be careful, okay?" Tristan meant it. After losing Illeana, he didn't want to lose Ryleigh, too.

"I will," she agreed. "And, I have Nissa."

The two held each other and didn't want to let go. Ryleigh was the first to end the embrace. Taking a breath, she turned around and headed off, ready for whatever might come her way.

22

The journey for lost souls

Tristan wasn't sure which direction he should go. With Vee on his shoulder, he walked into what seemed to be another dark hallway. The hallway, instead, was a doorway that opened into a very large room with additional exits on either side. The room was decorated almost royally and set up like a conference room. A large table sat in the center surrounded by gilded chairs lined with plush velvet. Although Tristan wasn't exactly afraid of anything that might be lurking, he was still very cautious crossing the room.

"Be wary," he told Vee.

"Yes, Master," Vee replied, knowing that in a moment's notice, hell could break loose.

Tristan wasn't sure which path to take, so he took the one that was closest to him – the path in the middle of the room. He felt a cool breeze come through the doorway. It caressed his skin and carried with it a scent that he could remember. Finar didn't keep him in his cell, he dragged him to Illeana's...but how far exactly did he drag him. The smell – he knew it. He felt he knew it from something. It was sweet and pungent. It brought back sadness into the center of his chest. He had to find out what it was and started to increase his pace. Hesitating, he peered around a corner, looking for anything or anyone. The pathway led to an avenue of cells that lined the walls. Door after door where Fae were kept during the times they were in hiding.

At the end of the hallway lay another dark entrance. Hearing a foreign noise, Tristan motioned to keep quiet. He thought he heard a muffled whimper coming from up ahead. Tristan switched to his form once they reached the end of the avenue so that he could see within the darkness.

He was able to make out four doors that were similar to the one he had in his cell: wooden with iron bars through it. He went to the window of the first cell and peered through. It was empty.

The next cell contained a figure that he couldn't make out. The third was empty and the fourth... twin girls. They had to be Sam and Cael's girls. Their cheeks were painted with dust and grime. Their eyes, tired and bloodshot, were not the sparkling azure gems they should be. Mucus-dried lips cried for moisture.

"I am going to get you out of there," Tristan reassured.

They were scared. He could see the fear in their eyes. He had forgotten what he must look like to them. But he also knew that they had to have known their parents' true forms and seen them at some point in their lives.

"I know your mom and dad," Tristan said.

"That's what the bad man said," said one of the girls, her voice low and scratchy.

"Yeah, that's what he said, and he brought us here," said the other girl.

Tristan thought for a minute. "I know that is what he said. I promise I am going to help you. I can't tell you to trust me, but would I tell you that if I were here to harm you?"

Tristan certainly didn't know if they would understand what he was trying to convey. He had to think through and take a look at the other noise he heard. He went back to the first cell. He saw the outline of a body.

"Hello?" he called out.

He heard a muffled sound.

"Are you okay?" he asked. He saw the figure move.

"Water," the voice called out.

Luckily, they had thought to bring water with them, "Just in case," Ryleigh had said. "It was always an essential anytime my parents and I did anything."

Tristan was now grateful for the suggestion. He reached into his backpack and then passed the water through the bars.

A haggard looking woman approached him. Although her face was gaunt, her natural beauty still shown through. Her stark green eyes shone brightly and seemed grateful for her thirst to be quenched.

Tristan looked at the woman carefully. The familiarity of the face was too uncanny. "Adrianne?" he asked.

The woman looked at him at first with shock and then fear, "Who are you?" she asked.

"I am here with Ryleigh, we were looking for you."

Adrianne approached the bars with urgency. "You need to get her out of here!" Her face was the picture of panic. She did not want her daughter anywhere in the Sanctum. There was too much danger and too much risk. "She cannot be here. Where is she?" she asked quickly.

"She took another path. She was looking for you and Tom."

Adrianne reached through the bars to grab Tristan's collar. "She is special, Finar wants her. He never knew...he never knew..." she trailed off.

Tristan looked at her earnestly. "She knows she was a twin."

Adrianne's eyes were wet with emotion. "Save the girls and go. I am too much of a burden. I am weak and I can't do anything. My imp... She is dead."

Vee heard her say this and allowed a high pitched sound to escape before clamping his long-fingered hand over his mouth.

"I am not going to leave you in here alone, we are all going together," Tristan remarked. "You may want to stand back."

"You can't do anything to these doors. They are resistant."

"Not to me they aren't. Now, stand back!" he ordered.

Adrianne moved to the farthest corner of the cell and waited. She wasn't holding her breath.

Tristan in his true form started to gather energy from the twin inside him. He opened the palm of his hand and started an energy globule. It continued to increase in size until it was the size of a softball. Tristan opened his eyes and launched it at the door's handle. The door splintered and fell off its hinges. Tristan entered the cell. "Come on, let's go." He reached out his hand to help Adrianne up from the floor. "We have to get these kids and find Ryleigh. She is looking for Tom, and I am not sure where Finar could be."

Adrianne seemed to gather all of her strength, as broken as she appeared, and walked out of the cell with Tristan. "Right, let's get these kids."

* * *

In the darkness, Ryleigh continued to look up to reassure herself the lights were not threatening to go out. It wasn't that she was afraid, but she was. She could feel her stomach continuing to perform gymnastics in her abdomen.

"It's okay, Mistress," Nissa reassured.

Ryleigh knew it would be okay. She continued to follow the inner compass that guided her. She wasn't sure where it was taking her but she was comfortable following it. She reached a fork. At this point, indecisiveness stepped forward. She wasn't sure which way to go.

"Just feel it," she told herself aloud.

She closed her eyes and listened. This was something she continued to practice with Nissa, listening with her mind and her body and paying attention to the signs that she received. She felt a whispering to her right. A whispering that pulled her more in that direction. It was the way she decided to go.   It seemed that, with each step, the pathway grew darker. She pulled out a flashlight, grateful for her family and their "list" ability. She wasn't quite sure where she was going, but it felt familiar to her.

Almost to her core. This was a place she was supposed to be and supposed to recognize.

* * *

Tristan, Adrianne, and the twins headed back the way that he'd come. Tristan could hear noises behind and to his side.

Adrianne looked wild-eyed. She felt naked without her imp, almost as if a part of her were missing. She yearned for her husband. It was the only way she could draw any power now. Although Vee worked his magic and attempted to heal her, it didn't make her complete and fill in the void she was currently feeling.

She had the girls to either side of her holding their hands. She could feel how afraid they were through their trembling fingers. "Shhh now, it will be okay. We will get you back to your parents."

Tristan still hadn't the heart to tell the kids that their parents were dead; however, he knew that he had to get them out of the Sanctum and away from Finar. He figured he would take them to the safe house and find someone to watch and keep guard over the children until another relative stepped forward. Finar hadn't scared the entire community…yet. He was powerful, but he wasn't powerful enough above ground.

They reached the room where Tristan imagined hearings or rituals taking place. His eyes drew upon the center of the room and he stopped – rigid.

In the center of the room waited Finar. Dressed in his debonair flair for style. "Now, now," he mocked in his haughty voice. "Where do you think you are going?"

Adrianne backed up with the kids.

"I am taking them out of here, Fin," Tristan said as his form emerged. The flames licked at invisible wind traveling over his body. He could feel Illeana's Chi raging inside of him. "You can't stop me," he threatened.

Finar laughed. "Oh really? You think I can't stop you?"

He launched a condensed ball of energy toward Tristan. Tristan jumped and rolled out of the way as it crashed into the wall behind him. He wasn't prepared for that. He would have to be quicker on his feet and reflexes.

Inside, he talked to Illeana. *You have to help me. I have to save these kids…and Ryleigh's mom.* He could feel the reassurance from Illeana and a well of power deepened within his core. Tristan created his own energy ball and hurled it towards Finar. Finar was fast. He moved out of the way quicker than Tristan could blink.

He saw Finar direct his attention toward Adrianne and the girls. Tristan put himself between them balling his fists and coercing the flames to the surface.

"You will not have them," Tristan spat. "And by the way, Illeana says 'Hello'." Finar looked amused as Tristan shot flames from his hands towards Finar.

The flames collided with Finar's chest, covering it like plated armor. Finar cried out in pain and fell to his knees. Tristan claimed a small victory and shot out another length of flame. The flame curled around Finar's abdomen and he doubled. Tristan looked back towards Adrianne and the girls. "Get out of here!" He pointed towards the hallway that he came through to find them.

Finar started laughing. Mia appeared beside him and the flame seemed to dissipate. Finar stood laughing at Tristan, "Oh, you are getting better. But, you will have to do much *much* better than that." He wiped off the dust from his arms, "You can inflict pain, but I am so much more than you, youngling."

Tristan was angry. He flung three more explosive energy bursts toward Finar who deflected them into the rock beside him. Tristan could feel the slivers of rock scrape and embed themselves in his skin, but he didn't care. He continued to barrage Finar with the anger resonating from within.

"You are a monster!" he screamed.

Vee pleaded with Tristan, "Master, stop, you are going to hurt yourself!"

Tristan started pulling energy through Vee, incapacitating him. Finar saw Tristan gearing up and flashed to his form. It was dark and sinister. His form had changed since the last time Tristan saw him. His eyes were glowing embers, skin as black as ice under a midnight sky. This was the result of consuming multiple Chi. He looked like a demon of old. Demon, no matter how labeled was still Fae. And Finar's form was one that children would be scared of in the middle of the night. Tristan's heart skipped a beat. He could see the power starting to coagulate in the palms of his hands. The room began to dampen with Finar's darkened energy stifling the oxygen in the room.

The twins streamed tears down their cheeks, and Adrianne seemed to just freeze as if she were a deer in headlights. She stared at Finar, vastly afraid as he continued to ramp up for his next move.

Tristan stood ready. He was ready to face him.

Finar flung a large black ball at Tristan. Instead of deflecting it, Tristan attempted to catch and absorb it.

The pain was excruciating. It tore through his limbs, setting fire through every pore. He screamed at the feeling of the heaviness from the energy. It left a dirty, grimy, metallic taste in his mouth. He tried to inhale and meld the Chi with his own. He heard Vee scream as he tried to pull it into himself. The twins started screaming loudly as the world crashed around him and went dark.

* * *

Ryleigh heard screams…at least she thought she did. Everything grew so quiet that she could almost hear her own heart beating through her chest.

She looked to Nissa. "What was that?" Nissa shook her head. "I don't know, Mistress, but it sounded very painful."

Although she was now permanently connected to Tristan, she couldn't feel him. Finar changed Tristan and Ryleigh was now more than a Halfling. She tried reaching out to try and find him, but the other pull she felt overtook her. She was determined to find her parents. It was important. She followed the winding path pushed by only her gut and intuition.

Coming around a corner, she hesitated. The air tasted different here, it was sweeter and felt more calming than in any other section of the Sanctum that she'd walked through. Ryleigh took a deep breath, inhaling her surroundings closing her eyes. She wanted to remember this. Nissa was also affected by the change. She hopped from Ryleigh's shoulder and started to walk along side of her. Ryleigh hesitated before rounding the corner.

She saw the room from her dream. The altar, the symbols, the paintings. It was all too familiar. She wasn't sure why, but she knew that she needed to be here. Ryleigh walked over to the altar and ran her hands along the smooth stone. There was energy here.

"Nissa, can you feel this?"

Nissa nodded in agreement. Ryleigh closed her eyes to listen to the hum beneath her fingers. The soft tones were an incantation singing her a lullaby. Ryleigh wasn't aware of it, but her body started to sway to the music she was hearing. It was almost as if it were a pulse beneath her fingers.

Nissa looked at her Mistress and started to get a little nervous. She wondered if this was a good place or a bad place. She tugged on Ryleigh's pants and pleaded, "Mistress?"

Ryleigh thought she heard and felt something, but all she wanted to hear was the slow drum beat and melodic tones of the music beneath her hands. She wanted to tap into it – just a little bit. Opening herself up, she allowed her energy to flow into the stone.

The stone began to glow an eerie incandescent yellow. Ryleigh opened her eyes feeling the change. She was pleasantly surprised and curious. The room increased in light and it flickered, beating in time with the energy in the stone. Nervousness rose to the surface within her and she could feel a rumbling inside.

Nissa was scared. She knew that something was wrong and this was not supposed to happen. Nissa was connected to this place and had genetic memories, this wasn't supposed to happen. At least, not with her here.

Ryleigh stepped back, afraid of what she might have done. She could feel others around her. She could feel other beings like her…but not like her, in the Sanctum. It was as if she was truly connected to this place.

Nissa was nervous. "Mistress?"

"Shhh," Ryleigh responded. "I'm trying to listen."

Nissa obeyed as she always would. She could feel what Ryleigh was trying to do. Ryleigh was reaching out and trying to see or feel what exactly or who exactly was around. All she could pick up were glimmers of beings that streamed through her consciousness.

She felt the screams. Her green eyes flashed open. "We have to go."

Nissa jumped on her shoulder and Ryleigh started to run in the direction she felt the screams emanate.

* * *

Tristan's consciousness slowly started awakening, and his body felt as if it were in an awkward position. His head was pounding, and his eyes felt as if there were splinters. But his body felt off. He knew he was on the ground. He could feel the stone beneath him. The warmth of the ground soaked through his clothing and drifted into his skin. As he became more awake, he was able to hear what surrounded him. He could hear the screams of the girls and the rage of a male voice. He knew it was Finar. He tried to slowly move separate parts of his body.

He heard Adrianne's voice echo in the distance. It was shrill with cries and pleadings.

"Tell me. Tell me about your daughter, Adrianne," he heard Finar ask.

"You know! You know already," she cried. Tristan heard the pain being inflicted on her.

The male tone was different, he wasn't sure if it was truly Finar. But then, he couldn't be sure of anything other than the splitting headache he was feeling.

He groaned, but the voices didn't stop. He was pretty sure that they did not hear him as he rolled over despite his bones and body protesting. But he kept thinking about the girls and Ryleigh's mom. He tried to pull energy from Vee to heal himself, but he couldn't feel him around. He knew that he had to be knocked out or unconscious, but he couldn't feel him at all. This worried him. He would look later, but for now, he needed to get up.

He opened his eyes and noticed that he was hidden behind a pillar. At least he wasn't dead. He took the opportunity to try to pull his body up from the ground. Leaning on the pillar, he could vaguely see Finar's shape holding Adrianne by the front of her clothes.

The girls were cowering against a wall huddled together. One of the twins spotted Tristan. Tristan placed his finger to his mouth motioning them to be quiet. He could tell that Finar was more invested in the conversation he was having with Adrianne. Mia was on Finar's shoulder just watching. It seemed there were other shadows behind Finar, supporting him. Tristan couldn't be sure since they were not visible, merely an echo of shapes whispering behind his coattails.

Tristan didn't want to shoot blind and hit Adrianne, she couldn't defend herself. Tristan felt the storm brewing within him and reached deep. He knew he couldn't absorb Finar's energy, but he could deflect it and dodge it - maybe. If he could catch him unsuspecting, then he might be able to save them all.

Tristan had to think. *Think Tristan, think.* He told himself. He reached inside, looking for his twin, knowing that she was there biding her time. He needed to draw from her strength and her desire to kill Finar.

He concentrated to listen for her. He listened for her melodic tones, the ones he recognized, that he could pull into his own. Although he was powerful, he didn't draw from Illeana prior to fighting Finar previously. He knew he needed Ryleigh also in order to completely incapacitate him. But at this moment, he needed to save her mother.

Illeana stirred inside of him, combining with his energy, and he started to ramp up. His form changed behind the pillar into something new and cruel. The hatred felt by him and Illeana changed his flames to black. A dark contrast to his violet colored skin. He felt the mass of energy through his palms, knowing that Finar could hurt and wanting to hurt him all the more. Tristan's emotion shifted and changed the density of his energy to something dark and cruel.

He waited. He wanted to bide his time to focus on the figure holding Adrianne. Closing his eyes, he used his mind's eye to concentrate on Finar. Opening his eyes, he could only see him. A direct shot. One shot. As he raised his hands in front of him, Mia spotted him.

Tristan did not hesitate. As if in slow motion, he launched the compiled Chi balls simultaneously toward Finar. Finar turned a half a second too late, they exploded into him, knocking him backward. Immediately, Mia jumped to Finar's side and faded him away.

Adrianne fell, crumpling to the ground like a falling stack of cards. The twins were behind her against the wall, eyes large as saucers. Tristan rushed to Adrianne's side.

Picking her up, Adrianne's body was weightless. Looking into her eyes, he could see something was wrong.

"What is it?" he asked her.

When she spoke, it was as if no breath formed the words. "It's too late."

"What is too late?" Tristan's voice pitched upward with worry. He saw the blood beginning pooling to the front of the shift she was wearing, changing its color from blue to a mottled purple tone. He reached down to inspect the wound and found a small dagger.

"I can heal you," he said reassuringly.

Adrianne shook her head. "No, no, it is my time to go. I have lost everything."

Tristan could hear her heart still beating strong. "You can live," he implored. "Ryleigh will be here soon," he consoled.

Adrianne offered a slight grin baring slightly pink teeth. Tristan knew it. He hoped that Ryleigh would show up soon.

His hand, still ahold of the handle of the blade. He attempted to move his hand away from the blade, but Adrianne held his hand in place.

"It needs to stay in for me to heal you," he said.

"No, pull it out, it's killing me faster." This meant the blade was enchanted with witch magic.

"But, you might die before Ryleigh gets here," he implored. Tears formed behind his eyes; he couldn't be responsible for the death of her mother. It made his chest ache for his own parents and his sister who was no longer with him physically. "I can't do it."

Adrianne nodded. "I will be okay for a little while longer. It has to come out. It has to."

Tristan knew this to be the truth, he had heard of bewitched blades and how they kill from the inside out. He could see it was already affecting her. Without warning her, he pulled the blade.

Adrianne cried out.

"I am so sorry, I'm sorry," Tristan continued to repeat. He placed his hands on the wound, willing it to close, but he knew they would not. He focused on the blood, attempting to staunch the flow. He succeeded – just barely, but he needed her to stay alive for Ryleigh.

Tristan stood with the blade in his hand. Intricate craftwork decorated the handle. But before he could dispose of it, he heard a cry.

"Mom!"

Ryleigh found them.

23

Whose fault is it really?

Ryleigh knelt at her mother's side. Blood poured from her wound. Ryleigh wasn't aware of who killed her mother...yet. Only that Tristan was holding the blade. Her mother looked up, gazing into Ryleigh's eyes. She opened her mouth to speak.

"Don't say anything, Mom, it will be okay," Ryleigh said through tears,, knowing that it wouldn't be okay.

Adrianne spoke in a faint whisper, "Ryleigh, I am so sorry."

Interrupting her Ryleigh said, "No, Mom, don't apologize, don't. You were going to tell me, you were, that's why we were going camping. So you could teach me. I understand, I do." Tears continued to roll down her cheeks as choking sobs dammed her throat.

Smiling at Ryleigh, Adrianne replied, "I will be with you always. Do what is right."

Adrianne placed her hand on Ryleigh's chest above her heart. Ryleigh felt a burning sensation in its place. She was trapped in a moment of pain and power as her mother ebbed her life force into her. Ryleigh, realizing what was happening, grabbed her mother's hand attempting to remove it. She couldn't speak and she couldn't do anything but hold her mother's hand as the burning continued to increase. Ryleigh opened her mouth to scream but no sound came out.

She heard her mother's voice in her head saying, "*It will be alright, accept it and the pain will go way.*"

Ryleigh screamed a silent NO as the pain continued to increase.

Her mother's voice again comforted, "*Accept it, my sweet, I love you always.*"

Ryleigh's sobs shook her body like a violent earthquake. She knew she needed to accept it and reluctantly she did so. The pain immediately subsided as a whoosh of energy flowed into her, breaking through every pore and making her skin glow. Her mother's hand dropped onto her lifeless body. Her vacant eyes staring into Ryleigh's. Ryleigh could only sit there are her mother's energy was consumed by her own. Eventually, she sensed someone behind her and stood up to turn around.

Tristan.

"You!" Ryleigh spat with venom. "YOU did this," she screamed as she edged closer to Tristan. Her emotions invaded her logic and she couldn't think straight.

"Ryleigh," Tristan said calmly as he moved towards her. "I did *not* do this. It was Finar. I swear." He pointed to her mother and the destruction around them. "I would never do anything like this. I could never *do* anything like this," Tristan pleaded.

Ryleigh started to feel the rage inside increase and pulled the energy from inside her. She formed cannonballs in the palms of her hands like she learned during training with Vera. They glowed a vibrant white and illuminated the rage in her eyes.

Tristan stared at her, pleading, "You don't want to do this, Ryleigh. I didn't do this; I did not kill your mother."

Ryleigh knew he was lying. She could see it in his eyes.

"Ryleigh!" Tristan screamed at her as she threw one of her energy balls at him.

"You *lied* to me!" Ryleigh spewed. Her anger darkened her features changing her into something different than what Tristan was used to seeing.

He quickly dodged the ball while simultaneously throwing his blue flames around him, forming a circle surrounding his body in a bubble. Ryleigh threw another ball at him, the energy ball bounced off of the barrier exploding into a wall beside her. Ryleigh could only see darkness surrounding Tristan. The anger changed her, making her think that everything she knew was a lie. She wanted revenge. .

Ryleigh geared up to throw another energy ball. She increased the mass of this one, thickening it, making it much denser than the one previous. She ignored Tristan's pleas. Tristan stood his ground as Ryleigh threw the mass. Instead of deflecting the ball; he pulled it inward attempting to transfer it to the barrier he created.

He fell to his knees. It was too much for him. "Ryleigh watch what you are doing?" Tristan pleaded one last time. "See the truth for yourself. I did not do this!"

Ryleigh projected another ball which increased to the size of Tristan's bubble. Before she could throw it she heard a familiar voice, "Ryleigh, he didn't kill your mother. It was my fault."

Ryleigh's energy fizzled out immediately. "Daddy?'

Ryleigh fainted.

* * *

Ryleigh's eyes flickered as she came to. The first face she saw when she opened her eyes was her father. At first she was happy to see him, she had been looking for him for so long and craved the interaction, but remembering what he said to her before she blacked out, she started to back away.

"No, no, Ryleigh," he said, grabbing hold of her. "You need to listen to me." Ryleigh stopped struggling and stared at her father inquisitively, hesitating, waiting for the words to come out of his mouth that would make everything okay. That he would take back what he said to her.

"It was my fault all along. Her becoming my mate is what started it. It was entirely my fault, Ryleigh."

24

A sad reunion

Ryleigh couldn't believe her dad was standing before her or her mother lying on the ground next to her. Her mother's body was a shell of what she was before fading into ash. She wasn't sure what happened, but there were twin girls behind her and Finar nowhere in sight.

Ryleigh shook her head. "I…we need to get out of here."

Tristan agreed, "We do, and I need to take these girls to the house."

Ryleigh looked at Tristan, remembering he was holding the blade. But also that she tried to kill him, "Why? Why do you have a knife?" she asked.

"Finar. He stabbed your mother with it. It is bewitched. The only way to stop the magic from killing her inside, is to remove it. She made me. And…" Tristan started to choke up with tears and

S. E. Myers

swallowed it back down. "She wouldn't let me heal her. She just wouldn't." A tear escaped and rolled down his cheek.

Ryleigh believed him and felt terrible. She could feel that he was telling the truth. His emotions carried the truth through her body.

"We need to get out of here," Ryleigh commented.

Tristan started looking around the room for Vee. He reached out to see if he could trace him with energy. He felt something close to the pillar where he was flung.

Running over to the pillar, he moved the rocks around that gathered from being shattered by the force of his body and found Vee. He was badly injured. There was still life force flowing through him. Tristan could hear the little pitter patter of his heart.

He could not heal him alone though, it took an imp. "Nissa! I need you! Please! Vee is hurt."

Nissa appeared next to Vee and looked at Tristan. She placed her small hand on Vee's wrinkled forehead. He looked so much older than he was. He was only seventeen, but imps aged twice as fast as Halflings.

Ryleigh came over and knelt beside Vee's fragile body. She sucked in her breath looking him over. "Will he be okay?"

"Yes, Nissa can heal him. He has a strong heart."

"Mistress, he will be fine," Nissa reiterated.

Ryleigh's father was in the background watching and standing with the twins. Ryleigh looked back at her father, just wondering what the future was going to bring.

Nissa started to channel energy using Tristan as a conduit. The color started to return to Vee's body and his breathing regulated. The purple tones to his skin seemed to brighten and he opened his beady little eyes.

Tristan blew out his breath, he wasn't aware he had been holding it. "I am so glad you are alright."

"Yes, Master, me too," Vee said and he stood up. He stumbled for a second and regained his balance. Tristan picked him up and put him on his shoulder.

He looked to the others. "We need to get out of here."

Ryleigh looked at the shell of her mother's body knowing it was now ash. "Let's go to the house."

Tristan and Vee faded with the twins. Ryleigh with Nissa and her father.

* * *

At the house, Ryleigh cleaned the girls and tried to find something to wear. Luckily, Illeana had been small enough in sizes and had clothes small enough to fit the girls. After their showers, Ryleigh gave them the shorts and t-shirts she'd rummaged.

Standing in the bathroom she looked at herself in the mirror. She thought she looked much older than her age. So much had happened in a short amount of time. She bent over the running sink and splashed water onto her face. She just needed to breathe for a moment.

Shutting and locking the door, she sat on the edge of the tub. She tried to put in order everything that she had learned and seen, but all she could see was her mother's face as she channeled her own life force into Ryleigh.

Ryleigh grabbed a towel from the rack, rolled it up, pressed her face into it and proceeded to scream. The scream turned to sobs erupting from the deepest part of her. Her body physically ached from the sadness and frustration she felt. She'd found and lost one of the most important people in the world to her, followed by the thought that Tristan killed her. The tears continued to smother the towel she held to her face.

A knock at the door startled her. "Ryleigh? Are you okay?" Her father's voice echoed through the door.

She wiped her face and stood up turning on the sink again. "Yeah, I'll be out in a minute. I'm just… cleaning up."

Tom didn't believe her, but he knew that she needed a moment to collect herself. As it was, he wasn't even sure where he was or what he was doing. He'd barely escaped with his life. He was torn between being reunited with his daughter and losing his life mate.

Ryleigh emerged from the bathroom, her eyes still swollen from crying. Tom reached out to her, but Ryleigh hesitated.

"Why didn't you ever tell me?" she asked.

Tom knew this was coming; he just wasn't prepared how to answer it. Swallowing he said, "We wanted to protect you. And, not – not saying anything seemed to be the only way to protect you."

"Protect me?" Ryleigh half shouted. "Had I known, I would have been able to start protecting myself from the beginning!"

Tom agreed, "You're right, you are. I am so sorry." Tom's eyes started to threaten to release the tears he was holding back. "I am just so happy to have you back."

Ryleigh could see the anguish in her father's face and couldn't bear to hold a grudge. She half ran and crushed him in an embrace. "I missed you, Dad, I thought you were dead."

"I know, sweetie, I know." Tom kissed the top of his daughter's head. "I thought I was dead, too. I didn't know how I was going to get out of there or find you again."

Ryleigh pulled away, looking seriously into her father's eyes. "How did you get out of there?" she asked.

Tristan also took interest and wanted to know what happened. He walked into the room after having a shower himself. He was still feeling a bit of pain and ache from being tossed against a marble pillar. "Yeah, how did you escape?"

25

Tom's story

"I was in the cell next to your mother. Fin continued to use her in order to get me to talk about you and give him information. See, you are different." Tom said.
Ryleigh interrupted, "I know. I am more than a Halfling." Tom looked a little shocked. "It was in Vera's diary, and we kind of pieced things together, "Ryleigh acknowledged.

Tom nodded his head and continued. "He'd had that witch. I don't even know how he brought her down into the Sanctum, but there she was, creating spells for him. "Unbreakable magic" he called it. He'd threatened to kill your mother so many times I couldn't stand it. I didn't want to give in, but he was and is, so *strong*."

"Your mother and I – we knew that we needed to get you away a long time ago. We could see the signs from the time you were small how special you were. You knew things that you shouldn't know. I don't know how many times that your mother and I tried to keep things away from you...including Christmas presents, but you would always know what was in what box without ever seeing."

Ryleigh smiled. She remembered the Christmas she told her parents they should just let her have the doll she wanted because it was already under the tree.

"It was very hard to keep secrets from you. Your mother and I didn't think anything of it, until one day, one of your little playmates from school became very sick." Motioning to Ryleigh, "Do you remember that?"

Ryleigh shook her head. "I don't. How old was I?"

"You were probably three or four, and I think her name was Allison. There wasn't any moment in your free time that you two were not playing together. One day, she started getting sick. Her parents took her to the doctor, but they couldn't figure out what it was."

"One afternoon, she was feeling well enough to come over and play with you. You were just sick to death because you hadn't been able to play with her. You wanted to fix her. So you decided to play doctor and fix her. Your mother heard you in your room tell her to just lie down like she was on an examination table. So she walked into the room to check on you both."

"You were healing her. It was just not possible at such a young age without an imp. To even know what to do. You know?" Tom continued.

"Allison had healed. She left the house better than she had ever been in her life. Her parents were shocked and wanted to know what we did, but we continued to insist that nothing happened. Then Allison told her parents that you made her all better."

"That's when they demanded to know the truth. I told them to take her back to the doctor. A few weeks passed and we didn't hear from them again. We moved. Immediately. We kept you home after that, remember?"

Ryleigh nodded. She had to beg to be put back into public school when she was a teenager. She always argued that she was a freak and recluse anyway, that she needed the social interaction to make her a normal person. Her mother always laughed and said she was the most *normal* person she knew. How far from the truth that was right now.

"When your mother was pregnant with you," he continued, "she was pregnant with twins, as it is for our kind. But something happened, and one of them, died…" Her dad looked forlorn when he said that. "But, the funny thing was, one day there were twins, the next, there was just you."

Tom looked lost in thought for a moment. His eyes glazed over. Ryleigh knew he was thinking about her mother. She reached out to console him. Tom smiled and said, "We love you, you know. We knew there might be something different about you. We were willing to sacrifice everything. This is why we left. We did not want people like Finar to get their hands on you. We didn't want the Elders involved in our affairs. "

Ryleigh reassured her father, "I understand. I really do."

"We were going to tell you when we went camping, and then the accident." Tom's eyes welled with emotion. "I thought we lost you. When Finar appeared—"

"Finar? What do you mean Finar?" Ryleigh demanded to know.

"He caused the accident."

26

The accident

Ryleigh was sleeping in the backseat of the truck, and her parents were having a random conversation. Adrianne and Tom were excited and nervous for this trip. They knew it was a long time coming, and it would be well worth the experience for Ryleigh. But also confusing with how much they needed to explain.

They'd driven for a few hours already, silently falling into their routines. From New Mexico to Yellowstone took about fifteen hours. Ryleigh loved driving through Colorado and seeing the mountains. The constant jostling of the car would always rock her to sleep, even when she was a baby.

They'd driven through to nightfall with Tom and Adrianne taking turns driving. The interstate was dark, and there wasn't much traffic. Rounding one of the many bends they came to expect on the trip, Tom noticed a strange illumination ahead. As they drove closer, Adrianne started to slow down, but it was too late. Finar was standing in the middle of the road in his true from. Completely embodied and surrounded by energy.

Pulling the car to a slow stop, Adrianne grabbed Tom's arm. They looked at each other not knowing what to expect. Ryleigh was still sleeping in the back of the car. Adrianne was able to pull some energy from Ryleigh to keep her sleeping just in case. If things went wrong, she would rather her be asleep than awake.

"I'll go," Tom said opening his door.

"No, wait!" Adrianne said hurriedly. "We don't know what he wants, or even how he found us."

"It doesn't matter," Tom said. "He found us now, and we need to deal with it."

Adrianne knew he was right. She listened to her husband and he stepped out of the vehicle.

"Both of you!" called out Finar.

Adrianne's heart lurched. She took another look at Ryleigh. Finar was unaware that she was in the back seat. He didn't even know that they had a child.

Adrianne exited the vehicle and stood beside her husband Tom. She started to grab for his hand and Finar appeared in-between the both of them as quick as a lightning strike and vanished.

Mia stepped forward from the shadows. The imp turned his palm upward toward the sky and motioned his fingers toward him. The car began to roll and pitch forward landing on its roof.

As he closed his fist, metal began to pop and crumble into itself. That's when he heard it: the girl. The imp cocked his head to his side and listened again. Yes, he was sure he heard it.

The imp came close to the vehicle and peered inside. Inside the car was a girl. When he flipped the vehicle and crushed it, part of the metal from the door pierced through her abdomen.

The imp grabbed the girl and pulled her through the window. He breathed her in and could tell she was quite powerful but not so controlled yet. He decided he would let her live. His master wasn't there, and he didn't much like all the bad things he was made to do. He moved her out of the way and continued to make the car explode. On the side of the road, Ryleigh cried out in pain. That is when Mia decided to tell Tristan.

He faded away to Tristan's location and brought him and Vee back.

When Mia appeared Tristan was taken aback and immediately thought that Finar was summoning him. "What does he want now?"

Mia shook his little head. "Nothing, you must come with me."

"Well if he doesn't want me, why should I come with you?"

"You just must come; I need help to save her."

Tristan was intrigued and agreed. They faded to the accident.

Mia pointed. Tristan looked at the imp to thank him, but by the time he turned around, he was gone.

27

Dreams never let you sleep

"I knew that you would be okay," Tom continued. "I'd ensured that if anything ever happened to your mom and I, that my sister would get you."

"I was put in the hospital," Ryleigh said. "I had some pretty bizarre injuries."

Tom's face darkened with anger.

"But I'm okay," Ryleigh reassured. "Aunt Vera was nice to me also."

"Mia brought me to Ryleigh," Tristan chimed in. He wasn't sure if he should say anything but decided now was as good of time as any. "She was severely injured. Vee and I saved her life."

"Yeah, but I'm okay now." Ryleigh paused for a moment and then changed the subject. "Dad? How did you get out of your cell?"

Tom hesitated, "He let me go. I don't know why he did it, he just did."

Tristan wondered, "Where were you?"

"I wandered all over the Sanctum. I was trapped. My imp was killed by Finar. I tried to find a way to release my wife and the twins. But, without my imp, I am useless. I heard the screams and headed back toward you. "

Ryleigh was suddenly overcome with exhaustion and could feel how tired her body was. Even though Nissa helped heal her, mentally she was spent. She needed a rest and needed to escape into the darkness for a while.

"I have to sleep," she told them.

Tristan and her father both nodded her way.

She stopped and hugged her dad. "I missed you."

She headed into the back of the house to find refuge from the current madness.

Ryleigh suffered a fitful sleep. She kept dreaming about her mom and the look in her eyes, the pleading for Ryleigh to just accept what was happening. Waking up multiple times, she even wondered why she closed her eyes. All she could see was the pool of blood beneath her mother's body.

She knew that her mother gifted her Chi to her, but it wasn't like Tristan. Tristan explained how he could feel Illeana inside of him. She couldn't feel her mother inside of her. It was impossible. She sometimes would talk to her twin since she'd found out that she had one. She knew that it had to have been boy. Although, with the twin girls, this meant that there was something different about them, too. Something eerie with the way they looked at you. Their eyes seemed to pierce through her soul.

Her dream took her back to finding Tristan with the knife. Instead of missing him and her father appearing, she killed him. She could feel that she reveled in it. She was enjoying making him afraid of her. It was as if she fed on it, completely, and it felt natural.

As if this was what she was meant to do.

She woke up covered in a sheen of sweat. The day was still bright and, although it felt as if she slept through the night, it had only been an hour. She was a little afraid of the darkness that she felt. It worried her. She wasn't sure if she could even talk to Tristan or her dad about it. Although, she knew he would possibly understand what she was going through.

Shaking the sleep off, she walked into a conversation that seemed intense.

"There isn't anything you can do, Tristan," said Tom. "You are like this forever. More powerful, stronger, this is why Fin wants you on his side and will not kill you. It's Ryleigh I'm worried about."

"What about me?"

They turned around, surprised to see her standing there; they were so involved that they hadn't heard her approach them.

Her dad stuttered for a moment, "H-hey! We thought you were still sleeping!"

"Apparently," Ryleigh said, sarcasm implied. "So, what *do* you mean then? I guess if you are worried about me, then I need to be worried about myself as well. Don't you think?"

Tristan crossed the room. He grabbed Ryleigh by her arms and pulled her close, "Of course you should be worried. You are different than me. You are more whole. I am..." Pushing her back to look in her face, "I don't know what I am. Can you feel another presence? You know...inside?"

"I can't feel my mom and haven't tried to feel my twin. I talk to it all the time but, I haven't tried to be honest. I wanted to, but I was afraid. I didn't want to know or feel that someone or...something else was inside of me. The thought of it really creeped me out."

Tom broke into the conversation, "Well, we can help. I mean, I can't. I don't know if I can connect with anyone else. It's been a long time."

"There's only one way to find out," Ryleigh announced.

28

The moment when all that didn't matter

disappeared

Tristan, Ryleigh, and Tom gathered in the living room after putting the girls down. Tom reached out to one of his contacts that helped him and his wife escape seventeen years earlier to find someone to take the girls. They would leave first thing in the morning to a safe place. Hopefully far enough from this madness. Not one of the three would be privileged to their location, nor would they know who took the twins. An imp would fade them out of the house and to a new location. It was for the twins and their own protection.

The all held hands, eyes closed. Tom was nervous as he hadn't connected with anyone but his wife in a very long time.

Ryleigh felt her father's nervousness and squeezed his hands. Concentrating on their breaths, Tristan and Ryleigh connected first. They'd decided that Ryleigh would attempt to stream Chi to Tom first.

She sent a small energy pulse to her father. She looked at him as he opened his eyes, feeling the electric sensation run up his arm. He concentrated on that feeling and tried pulling on it. He couldn't do it.

Tristan tried next. He sent a pulse to Tom. Again, Tom couldn't grab onto it or pull it. He dropped their hands.

"Well, I guess that's that," he said blandly. "To be honest, I'm okay with it."

Ryleigh broke her connection with Tristan and embraced her dad. "I love you."

"I love you too, honey," Tom replied. He would have to learn how to live life all over again as a human.

"Tristan and I will try later – to see if there is someone, or something inside," Ryleigh said.

Tristan nodded in agreement.

"Yeah, I'm sure you two will figure it out." Tom left the living room and went into the spare room he would be staying in.

"I think he'll be alright," reassured Tristan.

"I'm sure you're right," said Ryleigh. But she wasn't so sure.

* * *

Since the first time they connected, Ryleigh and Tristan didn't have an opportunity to really talk about what happened, or them… Or even touch. Too much transpired and interrupted their opportunity. Ryleigh wasn't even sure how she felt being connected to him, tethered to him. She did want it. Or something like it. From the time she was little, she had always craved for someone to be at her side. Which more than likely stemmed from the fact she was supposed to be a twin. So many times she talked to herself as if she was not herself, wondering if she was completely crazy.

Prior to meeting Finar face to face, she needed to talk to Tristan. She needed to experience that connection and feel inside that someone wanted and needed her just in case she would never feel it again and be sent spiraling headfirst into the nether. The thought of it bothered her immensely. She didn't want to be cast into a pot of melted energy that spiraled around forever. The explanation of the nether wasn't ever clear to any of them.

In the dark, she crept to Tristan's room, careful not to make any noise that would disturb the twins or her father. She opened his door gently, Vee was sleeping on the end of his bed and lifted his squirrely face and peered at her.

"Mistress?" he questioned.

Ryleigh stepped into the room. "Could I have a moment?" she whispered to Vee.

He cocked his head and looked hesitant to leave his master. "Go, Vee, go to Nissa," Tristan's baritone ordered.

Tristan looked as if he had been awake for a while; although, when she peered in the room, it seemed as if he were sleeping.

"I knew you would come," Tristan acknowledged. "At least, before tomorrow."

"Yes," Ryleigh answered. "I-I," she sighed. She tried to find the words to convey to him to let him know how she felt but there were none.

Tristan sat up cross-legged on his bed and patted the space before him. Ryleigh sat across from him. She was nervous and didn't know what to expect exactly. Neither did Tristan. What he felt that he needed to do came from instinct. Ryleigh was also led by that same instinct.

She reached out and placed her palm on his chest as they did before. Tristan did the same. Breathing in as the other breathed out. This time it was a little more intense and a little faster as they had connected previously.

Looking deeply and intently into his eyes, she thought she felt a stirring within her. She could drown in his violet eyes and their liquid pools of lavender. Once the connection was made, Ryleigh placed her hands on her legs. She was nervous about what might happen or come next. The temperature in the room seemed to have risen.

Tristan caressed the back of Ryleigh's neck. She allowed her head to fall into the palm of his hand feeling the warmth from inside. She could almost hear him, know how he felt. This was what she wanted.

Tristan pulled her to him. They'd become a little more in tune with their energy cycling to prevent anything from exploding, however, when Tristan pressed his velvety soft lips into Ryleigh's, her heart felt as if it were going to explode from her chest. His kiss was urgent and aggressive, as if he wanted to imprint his lips onto hers. Ryleigh felt the urgency herself. She wasn't sure if she was ever going to have this again.

Tristan pulled away staring at her. "I don't want to lose you."

Tears began to well in her eyes and she had to swallow a lump that was being created in her throat. "I don't want to lose you either, Tristan."

"This connection, it's more than just predetermined you know," Tristan said almost whispering. "I really do care about you. I would have cared about you even if we didn't have some stupid destiny planned for us genetically."

"I know. I feel the same way. I'd dreamt about you so many times before," she told him. "I know I've said it before, but, even though we are supposed to be matched for each other, I've always known it. Does that make sense?"

Tristan nodded. "I love you, Ryleigh."

Ryleigh's heart caught in her throat and she began to sob.

Tristan pulled her close into his chest, a place that knew her best. "Why are you crying?" He smoothed her hair back from her face and kissed her tears away.

"I don't want this to go away. I don't want to lose this," Ryleigh sobbed. "I finally have this, something I've searched for, and now tomorrow – it could be all gone."

"Hey now," he reassured, "you have been through so much already and come out on top. We are going to survive, and when Fin is dead, we can move on and restart our lives."

Ryleigh knew that Tristan was saying these words to reassure her. She could feel him running through her with his energy untamed like wild horses on the plains. She could feel the truth of the matter and that he was scared just like her. He was scared he would never see her again.

He kissed her deeply. He wanted to pull all of her inside of him so he could protect her. Grabbing her into a fierce embrace, they slept in each other's arms. Sleeping a dreamless sleep, unaware of what tomorrow would bring.

* * *

In the middle of the night, Ryleigh's cellphone rang. It was Cyrus's phone number.

"Hey there," Ryleigh mumbled through sleepiness.

"Well, hey there yourself," answered Finar cheerily. "Guess who I have?"

Ryleigh shot out of bed waking Tristan. "What's wrong?" Tristan asked.

Ryleigh waved him off and answered, "What have you done?"

"Oh, don't worry, I won't kill your friend or his mother – yet. You need to come and visit me. Tomorrow. Six p.m. Via the portal at your aunt's mansion."

"Or what?" Ryleigh asked, scared.

"Do I even have to say it?" Finar rebuffed.

"No," said Ryleigh. "I'll be there."

"Good, good," said Finar. "And bring Tristan, too."

Finar hung up and Ryleigh turned to Tristan. "He has Cyrus."

29

Preparations are a witch

The morning came too quickly despite everybody's fitful bouts of restless sleep. Ryleigh woke her father after the conversation she had with Finar. Her dad promised he would try to get as much help as possible.

Tom had an announcement for them after they discovered the twins were gone.

"I've found us a witch."

"What do you mean you found us a witch?" asked Ryleigh.

"If we are going to go up against Finar, we might need one," said Tom matter-of-factly. "I've used the last of my savings to bribe her."

The witch hated Halflings and Fae born. In order to help, she had to be bribed handsomely to assist and was a just-in-case factor. If they needed her, they would summon her. The witch was more than content to be "Plan B". She wouldn't return the bribe even if she was never used. Just being around them all was close enough for a death sentence.

"Also, I am going to go with you both," confirmed Tom.

"No, you're not," Ryleigh tried to protest.

"Yes, I am," said Tom. "You two might need someone else there, and although I can't do much," Tom pulled a .45 Colt from behind him, "I can still use this."

Ryleigh's mouth dropped open and Tristan smiled broadly.

"But –" Ryleigh began.

"But nothing," interrupted Tom. "I am going and that's that."

Arguing Tom's point was moot. He was going to go and she would do her best to keep him safe.

* * *

They were as prepared as they were going to be.

They were on their own. Tristan – the more than a Halfling, Ryleigh – the whole Fae, Tom – the contributor, and Katelyn – the solitary witch. Finding Katelyn was a blessing and a curse.

Ryleigh and Tristan had been practicing their instant connection and using that to increase their power.

On their own, Tom tried connecting with Ryleigh again and discovered he was able to connect to the part that Adrianne gifted her. It was a small part and only worked if they really concentrated on it. If needed, he would try to use that to his advantage. It would take all of them to take Finar down.

Nissa, no longer the baby she was only a few weeks ago, was ready, too. She had become one of the strongest imps because of Ryleigh. Even Vee was impressed with her.

Ryleigh went back over her list again with the group.

Laughing Tom said, "You and your mother with those lists. Couldn't go anywhere without ensuring that it was checked off multiple times."

Ryleigh rolled her eyes. "This could be life or death, so I am going to go over this for *my* sanity before we even think about stepping foot out of the door."

Tristan squeezed her around the waist. "I like it. Keeps us organized."

"See, someone appreciates that over-obsessiveness that I have."

The list was also keeping Ryleigh mentally in check. Keeping her mind focused on the smaller tasks instead of the bigger one helped her not be so nervous.

"So, Finar is expecting me. He has Cyrus and his family, knowing he was my only best friend." She choked up a little bit remembering the last conversation they'd had.

They had video chatted the week prior. Ryleigh was remiss with catching up with him, but she felt that she needed to tell him how important he was in her life.

"What's going on with you?" Cyrus had asked her.

"Nothing. Why?"

"Because, you're different. You're not how you were before."

Ryleigh didn't want to offer an explanation. He wasn't even aware that her parents had never died in the accident, or anything about her heritage or what she even was. She chalked it up as having to grow up more quickly. She promised to log onto their game that weekend before they signed off.

"Cy, you are my best friend. I want you to know how much I care about you," she reminded him.

"I know," he'd said before he logged off.

That was enough for her that he knew how she felt even after the incident at his house. She never did offer him an explanation for that. He thought that it was hormones and that he just wasn't feeling well.

Now she had to save him. And hopefully, Finar wouldn't kill him to spite her. Her dad thought that Finar wanted her, wanted to absorb her, but the Elders had reassured her it was impossible. They all knew about her now. They knew who she was and they were afraid.

Remembering their faces, hidden from her view so she could never know who they were, she shuddered.

"You are the first of your kind in a long time," one said to her in a Southern accent.

"Where there is one, there will be more," said another who sounded as if she were from New York.

They knew the danger of Finar but were powerless to stop him. That is why they didn't lock her up. She knew that. It ticked her off to no end that they would use her. She was afraid that, once Finar was locked up or destroyed, that they would put her away too.

Finar had free run of the Sanctum and was recruiting a large following. Ryleigh was afraid that this small rag tag crew would not be enough. Hopefully, with the witch, they should be okay. With Nissa and Vee, they could summon large quantities of Chi to help. To think, just a few months ago she was oblivious to all of this, and now... Now her life changed forever.

30

The final battle

Reaching the wreckage of Vera's mansion was disheartening to Ryleigh. She couldn't dismiss the fact that this was her home for a time. Remembering how Vera died, she wanted Finar to pay for that.

Tristan could feel the rumble with her and placed a hand on hers wrapping his fingers and sending a small pulse of warmth up her arm.

"It will be okay. We're almost there," Tristan said squeezing Ryleigh's arm.

She was prepared. She was pissed. She was ready. Nissa popped in beside her. "Mistress, Fin is there. He has others with him."

Tristan grimaced at the sound of his name. Ryleigh nodded. "I am sure he knows we are coming. He has to know."

Tristan pulled up outside the house. Ryleigh took a deep breath. She knew they were stronger than anyone that Finar could have recruited, but together they would need to confront Fin. He wasn't just half-Fae, he was something else and he scared the crap out of Ryleigh.

Her imp alighted on her shoulder. "Mistress, don't worry I will be here." Ryleigh knew she would be there.

Vee was in the back of the car asleep. Tristan wondered how he could sleep at a time like this, but he also knew that he was preparing.

"We need to stick together," Tristan reminded Ryleigh. "No matter what happens, we can't do it alone. Otherwise we are dead."

Ryleigh nodded. "I know."

"They have your friend Cyrus, and I know that. But no matter what, Ry, don't let him goad you." Tristan knew that Finar would probably use Cyrus to draw Ryleigh out.

This was going to be difficult. He wasn't even sure if they were going to live. They approached the house slowly, cautious. They were going through the front door. Tristan grabbed Ryleigh's hand and squeezed, reassuring her that he was there.

The plan was for Ryleigh and Tristan to enter the mansion first. Tom would come later. He was parked a half a mile away. Ryleigh had her cell phone in her pocket and on speaker-mode so that Tom would be able to hear everything going on. Vee and Nissa would get Cyrus and his mother out of the Sanctum as quickly and quietly as possible.

Taking a deep breath, Ryleigh reached for the handle and opened the door. Tristan and Ryleigh entered hesitantly looking around. Knowing the floor plan was a huge advantage for the pair. They went to the study to access the hidden room containing the portal below the house where Fin would be waiting for them. It seemed too easy.

It was abnormally quiet in the house, even the normal creaks and moans seemed to have ceased. The air crackled with intensity.

Ryleigh pressed the button underneath the desk, and the panel that she found before swung open from the wall. Tristan and Ryleigh headed down the stairs to the portal that would take them to the Sanctum. The pair desperately hoped that the cell phone would work where they were going.

Although they were going willingly now, they had a plan.

* * *

The Sanctum seemed darker this time around. "We need to stick together," Tom reminded them. "Where did he say he would be?" he asked Ryleigh.

Ryleigh looked at the phone. "He said to meet him where my mother died."

There was only one way in and one way out into that part of the Sanctum. "I remember how to get there," said Tristan.

Ryleigh nodded, "Yeah, I think I do too."

They didn't want to fade there, that would make it too easy. Instead, they wanted to scope out and see what was happening. Ryleigh wanted to feel the Sanctum. It used to be a place for their kind to come and be reenergized. It was beautiful. Her dad had explained that the Sanctum was another world filled with different creatures and amazement.

The Sanctum was just that – sanctuary. There seemed to even be a slight breeze that caressed the senses. Ryleigh felt energized just coming here. She could even feel Tristan relax next to her. Although the air smelled unique, it was a place that she could see herself coming back to. If Finar were abolished. Destroyed. Killed. Punished for all that he had done.

Ryleigh could feel the anger welling up inside of her.

They approached the room where Adrianne died. With each step, Ryleigh could feel the apprehension gaining strength within her.

Tristan grabbed Ryleigh's hand. "It's okay."

* * *

When they entered the room, Finar was waiting for them with a few of his 'closest' friends. It seemed as if he gained a following.

"Why, thank you for joining me," Finar said, motioning at two men guarding the entrance. They grabbed Tristan and Ryleigh from behind, restraining them.

"Wait! We are here as you asked," Ryleigh said sternly.

"Yes, yes. You're here. I'm here. We're all here," Finar said snidely, pointing to each of them and rolling his eyes. "It's time we get on with it, don't you think?"

Tom rushed into the room behind him, Katelyn trailing not far. Pointing his .45 at Finar he commanded, "Let them go!"

Finar started laughing; a deep laugh that echoed throughout the chamber. "Are you kidding me?" he said. "Do you honestly think that will keep me from doing you harm?"

Tom fired a shot at Finar. In one quick flash, Finar captured the bullet in an energy ball. Eyes glinting mischievously, he threw it, killing Katelyn instantly.

Tristan flashed into form and attempted to launch a counterattack. Finar deflected the cannons the young man threw.

Tristan escaped his captor and started running toward the back of the room to gain momentum. This gave time for Finar to create a larger mass. Vee appeared next to Tristan as Finar launched his energy web, trapping them both. The mass collided with their bodies flinging them toward the large pillars rendering them both unconscious.

Finar grabbed Tom by the throat. "You were very stupid," he remarked.

Ryleigh could see her father starting to lose consciousness. "Dad!"

"Didn't I warn you Ryleigh?" The words fell from Finar's lips, poisonous. "You and Tristan, no one else."

With Katelyn dead, Tristan unconscious, and her father incapacitated, Ryleigh didn't know what to do.

"Yes," she whispered, "I'll do what you want."

Finar smiled crookedly, evilly, his eyes glinting with satisfaction. "Good. If you don't want to lose your friend, you will listen to me. Come here." Finar threw her father into the rubble next to Tristan.

Ryleigh winced. "No!" she screamed as she ran at Finar attempting to punch him. He knocked her into the ground face first, and motioned for one of the guards to grab her.

"Sit," he commanded, pointing at the chair in the center of the room.

Ryleigh closed her eyes, silently praying for whatever was going to happen to happen quickly.

"Sit!"

Ryleigh sat down in the chair. A man and woman appeared on either side of her from the shadows, tying her to the chair's arms.

"What are you going to do to me?" Ryleigh questioned.

"I am going to take your energy into me," Finar said matter-of-factly.

"So, you're going to kill me."

"Yes," Finar replied. "I guess I am."

Ryleigh took a deep breath, attempting to stop her heart from feeling like it was beating its way outside of her chest. She knew the only way to save everyone was to sacrifice herself. She'd known when they began this treacherous mission.

Licking her lips she asked, "Will it hurt?"

Finar approached Ryleigh and caressed her head. "Yes, it will hurt. Would you like something to numb the pain?"

"No. No I don't want anything." She was determined to go out with a bang, regardless how much pain it threatened.

"You are a brave one, aren't you?" Finar laughed and motioned to the witch he'd summoned in. "Are you ready?" he asked her.

"Yes," she said.

"Then let's begin."

Finar had another chair brought in front of Ryleigh and sat down. He cocked his head to the side and looked at her face. She had a laceration above her brow and her nose was bleeding; bruises were beginning to appear under her eyes.

Ryleigh thought for one moment he might change his mind. His eyes looked almost caring.

He blinked away that possibility and said, "This will hurt less if you just give into it."

Ryleigh closed her eyes and reached out to see if she could feel her dad or Tristan. Nothing. Not a glimmer.

"I'm ready," she said.

Finar scooted his chair closer. He moved her knees between his, leaned in, and placed both hands on her chest. "Mia," he said. Mia stood between them, placing a hand on either one of their legs. Next, he called to the witch, "Now."

The witch began murmuring an incantation, creating a binding circle around the three.

Ryleigh felt an instant disconnect from her surroundings. It was as if she were a part of, and separate from the Sanctum. She heard a humming, distant but close. She wasn't sure if it was Finar's Chi, her own, or the Sanctum surrounding her. Feeling the heat of Finar's hands, she continued to expect a jolt of pain to rip through her chest at any moment. The anticipation within her was chomping at the bit.

Slowly, the heat began to spread from Finar's hands and into her chest. She felt a tugging within her chest as his Chi attempted to connect with hers.

"Oh – so – gently," Finar whispered.

Finar planned to make this extraction go as smoothly as possible. He could hear the tittering of voices surrounding him. His followers were watching, mesmerized. Soon, he would be in full control and no one and nothing could stop him.

The connection between Finar and Ryleigh made her jump in her chair as high as the bindings would allow. It wasn't painful – at first. She felt a small tingling sensation begin to build that started with her heart and resonated slowly through each of her limbs.

Finar continued to tug on her Chi, Mia helping with the connection. It grew faster and more impatient.

The stronger it pulled, the more painful it became. The tingling grew to a burning sensation covering Ryleigh's skin. She felt as if she were on fire and couldn't contain the pain anymore. She opened her mouth to scream, but it was silent.

Her brain was on fire, and she couldn't think. Her thoughts flashed only to the pain she was in. And then...

Ryleigh remembered her mother. Her Aunt Vera. Illeana. Her father. Tristan. Cyrus.

The images of those she loved flashed in her mind. Their faces. Her last memories. All of a sudden, the pain didn't matter. She realized she was connected with Finar and as he was pulling from her, she could do the same to him.

As soon as she realized this, she felt Finar shift in intensity. He realized her subconscious was still awake and Ryleigh might fight him. He started to draw on her Chi with more fervor.

Ryleigh opened her eyes. The anger and hatred she felt toward this man in front of her overcame all of her senses. She started to pull, using Finar's physical connection to her against him.

Finar's eyes flashed open and for a moment, she saw panic within them.

As she attempted to pull from him, she was met with resistance. It was as if she was trying to pull her hands from cement that was hardening. Ryleigh was not going to go down without a fight. She reasserted herself and pulled harder, attempting to block Finar's attempt to drain her dry.

She saw the shimmer from Finar's skin as he began to change into his form. His glowing red eyes peered into her soul as he forced his thoughts, *"Don't even think about it, child. You don't stand a chance."*

Ryleigh stared him down pushing her thoughts toward him, *"We'll see."* With that, she flashed to her form using the remnants amount of energy she had left. As soon as she did, she felt more powerful, more in control. The connection between herself, Mia, and Finar was more apparent.

The flow of energy from her to Finar was still trickling out.

Ryleigh closed her eyes and felt for any sign of Tristan. The barrier made it virtually impossible to feel anything outside of the circle they were bound. There was a tugging in the back of her mind, a small glimmer of something, she reached for it.

It was Tristan.

He was beginning to wake up. She could feel that, although he was beginning to regain his consciousness, he wasn't fully aware of where he was. The only way for her to make a connection was to break the resistance she was pushing toward Finar. A calculated but necessary risk.

She gripped the arm of the chair, the bindings still holding her in place. She could feel the confidence of Finar emanating from his blackened skin. At least she would die trying.

She released the resistance and immediately felt the excruciating burn and outflow of her Chi. Finar threw his head back and roared.

Trying to block out the pain reverberating through her head, she searched for the glimmer that was Tristan. Finar pulled her Chi with more intensity. Her form began to dissipate with the continuous stream of her Chi moving outwardly. She felt dizzy and was losing track of her own consciousness.

Please! she thought.

She gave one last push to search for Tristan. One last push, leaving her mind open and vulnerable.

* * *

Tristan turned his head side-to-side, his ears were still ringing from the energy bomb Finar threw at him. He felt a tingle in his mind that seemed familiar.

Ryleigh?

Tristan's body screamed at him with each movement he made. He hadn't felt pain like it in his life. The tingle came back, stronger, insistent. Tristan glanced around the room. Ryleigh was tied to a chair in the center of the room, her form ever present and glowing. Finar, in his own menacing form, was sitting across from her with his hands on her chest, and Mia in the middle connecting the two. A witch was in the background chanting. Ryleigh's head had fallen with her chin on her chest, her form fading.

The tingle came back, and Tristan reached for it, making the connection. As soon as he did, he could feel Ryleigh reaching through to him. Two words whispered through his mind before he blacked out, "*I'm sorry.*"

* * *

Ryleigh felt Tristan make the connection. Sending him an apology would not be enough for what she was about to do.

Using all the strength she could muster, Ryleigh began to pull. She felt his willingness to help her and hoped he would forgive her; she wasn't even sure that she would be able to do what she needed to do. It was a dangerous decision.

Through Tristan, Ryleigh was now connected outside the bound circle. But, so was Finar. She prayed he was too busy attempting to drain her so that he wouldn't pay attention to what she was about to do.

Without thinking about it, she pulled Chi from Tristan to aid in regaining her strength. She remembered when she touched the altar in the other part of the Sanctum and knew she could use its energy. She tried to remember that hum and used the connection with Tristan in an attempt to engage it.

The witch stopped chanting when she began feeling a rumbling beneath her feet.

One of Finar's lackeys yelled at her, "Keep going!"

It was faint, but she found it. The heartbeat of the Sanctum. The ebb and flow of energy beneath them giving each of them strength. Ryleigh tapped into it, using Tristan almost like an imp. With each beat, the energy flowed from Tristan into Ryleigh. She could feel her strength beginning to return, and then she could feel fear. Finar's fear.

She raised her head, slowly. She wanted to look him in the eye one last time.

Staring at him she sent him one last thought, *"Good bye, my dearest uncle."*

Before he had time to react, she slammed him with the energy she pulled from Tristan. Using him as a direct conduit to the heart of the Sanctum's energy. Tristan's body lifted off the ground, glowing an incandescent green. Finar's form started shifting and changing multiple colors. Black. Red. Yellow. Green. His eyes open wide. Still burning their fiery red, now filled with fear instead of contempt.

Mia attempted to remove himself from the connection but was caught in-between the struggle. The room started to shake and quiver and the ground rippled from the effect.

Finar's witch stopped chanting and stood wide-eyed at the scene playing out before her. She, along with Finar's followers, started running out of the chamber, attempting to leave the Sanctum. Stalactites lining the ceilings of the exits started crashing around them rendering them unconscious, or dead.

Ryleigh continued to feel the open tap of energy flow into her and stood up, strengthened. Her form reflected the iridescent glow of the Sanctum. She disconnected the contact between Mia and herself but left the connection between her and Finar. Mia collapsed, breathing heavily, nearly unconscious.

"You will NEVER be able to harm another one of us again," she forced into Finar's thoughts.

She released the flow of energy between herself and Tristan, and he dropped to the ground with a resounding *THUD*. Grabbing

Finar's hands from her chest, she pushed him back and forced him to his knees. Connecting directly to the Sanctum's power, she could feel the thrum and heartbeat matching her own. Her anger her ammunition.

With every beat, she continued pushing the energy into him. She could feel the intensity overwhelm him. She increased the amount of energy burning him from the inside.

Finar fell to the ground, writhing in pain. Ryleigh stood above him, her hands outstretched, now concentrating the energy she was pulling from the Sanctum and shooting it into his chest. She was going to kill him.

Tom, lying in the rubble against the far side of the room opened his eyes. "Ryleigh," he cried out.

She didn't hear him. She only had one mission; to rid the world of the menace preying upon the innocent.

Finar's skin began to char and smolder, filling the room with the smell of burnt flesh and hair. His mouth hung open, locked in an eternal silent scream. Ryleigh continued to push as much energy as she could into Finar, feeling his life force dissipate.

Tristan began to regain consciousness again. Holding his head, he saw Ryleigh standing over something in front of her. Tristan was weak, and every nerve in his body felt on edge.

"Ryleigh," he called out to her, barely an audible whisper. Tristan saw Tom crawling along the floor toward his daughter.

Ryleigh couldn't feel Finar anymore. The thrum of power was almost addicting and fed a need inside her, but instead of giving in, she backed it off.

She gazed down at the blacked corpse that lay at her feet. "Ryleigh," she heard the voice of her father and turned. He was edging toward her, crawling on the floor.

She could still feel the hum of the Sanctum coursing through her veins, through her entire body. She took a breath, regaining her composure, stopping the floor of energy into her, and changing from her form.

Almost immediately, her legs gave out from under her. Falling to her knees, Ryleigh grabbed her head trying to control the pounding from within.

Reaching out for an embrace, Tom said, "It's okay, honey. You did good. You did fine."

The room was in shambles. Tristan lay on the ground and attempted multiple times to lift himself, but he was unable to. "Help me," he cried out.

Ryleigh and Tom helped each other from the floor and made their way to Tristan. Ryleigh gazed around the room and saw Katelyn's body. She felt remorse for the poor witch – she never stood a chance.

"Vee! Nissa," Ryleigh called for the imps.

"I – I don't know where they are," Tristan said painfully.

Ryleigh sat down next to Tristan, smoothing his hair back on his head. "I'm sorry."

"I know." Tristan managed a half-smile. "I heard you. I don't remember or know what happened, but I am in a LOT of pain right now." Tristan groaned as he attempted to shift his body into a more comfortable position.

The three waited for what seemed an eternity when they heard a 'pop' behind them.

Ryleigh broke into a large grin, "Nissa!"

"Mistress," Nissa echoed Ryleigh's excitement.

"Where's Vee?" Tristan asked.

"At the house. He's recovering," Nissa said.

"Cy? His family?" Ryleigh asked.

"Safe," Nissa responded.

"Can you take us," Ryleigh asked.

Ryleigh didn't have to finish her sentence before Nissa faded them from the Sanctum.

31

Is this really the end?

Because Finar's witch gave Cyrus and his mother a spelled potion- they were unable to remember what happened to them. Tom convinced the family that Ryleigh went to visit Cyrus, and when she noticed they didn't answer the door, Tristan broke it down and rescued the family. Creating a carbon-monoxide diversion was the best idea they could come up with. They'd filled the house with carbon monoxide, broke down the door, and left the family outside to wake after calling 9-1-1.

Cyrus and his mother were sent to the hospital to recover and Ryleigh met them there.

"I don't remember saying you were going to visit," Cyrus asked Ryleigh as she stood by his bed in the hospital legitimately worried.

"We never talked about it. I was just going to show up," Ryleigh insisted.

Cyrus gave her a look she knew all too well. He wasn't convinced and had suspected something was off for a long time. As much as she didn't like the idea, she'd silently decided that she needed to truly distance herself from her friend and would allow a natural progression of separation help it along.

After her visit with Cyrus and his mother, Tristan, Ryleigh, and her father went back to the safe house to recuperate.

* * *

It only took a couple days before Ryleigh wanted to return to the Sanctum and visit Finar's 'office', a cubby hole littered with paperwork and filing cabinets. They saw the map littered with stick pins showing where Ryleigh lived; where Tristan and Illeana lived; where a dozen and more potential Halflings lived. Ryleigh could only imagine how many other children there were in the world who didn't know who they were.

Tristan, although still battered and bruised, was going through filing cabinets. He found Ryleigh's file. It was a copy of what was in Vera's home. Thumbing through it, he was not surprised to see pictures of her growing up, her parents, and copies of receipts from the planning of the camping trip.

"You might want to see this," Tristan called to Ryleigh. There had to have been at least twenty more files with names. "It looks like there were more plans for these kids."

Tristan turned to Ryleigh, "You know that he isn't dead." Ryleigh nodded. When Nissa and Vee went back into the Sanctum, his corpse was gone. "He will be back for us. For you. For them."

Ryleigh knew. She knew deep inside that she would see him again. And this time, she would be more prepared. But for now, she was content to start her life again with her dad, Tristan, and Nissa.

18677539R00148

Made in the USA
Lexington, KY
19 November 2012